THE SMUGGLERS OF BUENAVENTURA

by S. R. Van Iterson

translated from the Dutch by
Hilda Van Stockum

192 pages

for ages 12-up

$5.50 trade, $4.81 library

Publication date: 4/10/74

THE SMUGGLERS
OF BUENAVENTURA

By the Same Author

The Curse of Laguna Grande
Pulga
Village of Outcasts

THE SMUGGLERS OF BUENAVENTURA

S. R. VAN ITERSON

Translation from the Dutch by Hilda van Stockum

William Morrow and Company New York 1974

Printed in the United States of America.

1 2 3 4 5 78 77 76 75 74

Library of Congress Cataloging in Publication Data

Iterson, Siny Rose van.
The smugglers of Buenaventura.

SUMMARY: A young boy tracks weapon smugglers in the Columbian jungle.
[1. Colombia—Fiction] I. Title.
PZ7.I9Sm [Fic] 73-17723
ISBN 0-688-20116-4
ISBN 0-688-30116-9 (lib. bdg.)

CONTENTS

THE SMUGGLERS OF BUENAVENTURA

I

LING PA'S LITTLE LOT

Clouds hung low over the jungle, which spread along the entire coast. In the green shadows of the hot, moist, gloomy forest, numerous broad and narrow rivers, creeks, and swamps entwined themselves into an intricate labyrinth of waterways. The complicated pattern of deltas and islands made up a lonely wasteland.

A ship coming in from the sea tacked between sand-banks and cliffs and entered the wide, leaden waters of Buenaventura Bay. Above the mangroves on either bank the heat quivered. At the end of the bay, where the many rivers met, the town of Buenaventura lay deserted in the heat. Looking forlorn between sky and water, it lay clasped in the green grip of the jungle.

Roberto walked along the highway to Cali, the only road that connected Buenaventura with the mainland. He was on his way to his father's factory where shrimps and fish were frozen. It lay at the edge of the Dagua River. Like the other factories and dilapidated small shops, it was built on piles and jutted far out over the tidal silt strip, which was only dry during ebb tide.

As usual, a crowd of men and women stood at the entrance, waiting for the work that would begin as soon as the boats were in. Meanwhile, they were chattering to pass the time, their voices sounding shrill in the quiet of the afternoon.

In the factory corridor black girls stood washing shrimps. Roberto walked past them to the pier behind. His eye ran over the fishing boats moored there. "No luck," he muttered.

He had hoped to find the boats of old Josué at the landing stage, but he saw with one glance that they had not put in yet. His hands in his pockets, Roberto stood on the pier, waiting. He saw one boat being shifted. Another was unloading shrimps. A third was getting ready for departure. A muscular black man with a dirty towel knotted around his loins was spraying the deck. Two others, in faded shirts and patched trousers, carried baskets of ice aboard the boat, which lay low in the water. The baskets of ice were sent slithering along the wet deck and were caught by a lean brown boy. He poured the ice into four tanks under the deck, kicking down the shavings that escaped with his bare feet. During the voyage shrimps were kept fresh under ice in those tanks.

At the end of the pier lay a fishing smack with the grand name of *Esperanza.* A young black swung himself from its deck onto the pier. "*Ola,* Roberto, how are you? What's the news?" he asked.

"Good afternoon, Magdaleno. I came to see if old Josué had arrived with his boats. He's been gone more than ten days. I was sure he'd be in today," answered Roberto.

Magdaleno slowly rubbed his flat palms over his sweating, naked torso. "Perhaps he had bad luck like us," he said. "Who knows?"

"Did you have bad luck?" asked Roberto.

Magdaleno grimaced. "Bad enough," he said. "We have to go back right away with another boat to Panama for repairs. We've only just arrived, but that old money-mad devil chases us as if we were a school of fish."

"Who? The captain?" asked Roberto curiously.

"No, hush! I mean Gomez, the owner of *Esperanza.* He says he doesn't buy boats to have them stay ashore. Look, there he is, the old money monger."

Roberto turned around.

Against the wall of the factory, near the scales, stood a small fat man in an immaculate white suit. With gimlet eyes he watched the baskets of shrimps, which were being unloaded from one of his boats. Every time a basket was placed on the scales, he hastily wrote down its weight in a greasy little notebook. His sharp eyes glittered greedily. He looked up when he felt Roberto's gaze on him.

"Well, I'm off," said Magdaleno hastily.

Roberto sauntered away from the pier and mounted the narrow wooden stairs to the attic of the factory. An old Negro with gray, curly hair was mending nets. He scarcely glanced up.

It was comparatively cool in the attic. The roof rested on concrete posts, and the wooden walls between them were not a yard high. The wind could circulate freely, and there was a broad view. Leaning with his elbows on the wooden partition, Roberto gazed across the river. The water was shot with weird yellow tongues because of the silt it carried in its voyage from the mountains. Several hours ago the tide had turned, and the water was flowing back to the sea. Roberto could see the slimy roots of the trees along the Dagua River emerging into view. On the islands downstream, among the mangrove bushes, the soil was already drying under the pile dwellings. The air roots of the mangroves rose like wet, twiggy arms out of the water. A long canoe was gliding silently into this still, green world.

From the factory attic Roberto could see Buenaventura lying in a haze of green. It was a little town, built on an island, at the meeting place of many rivers. Mainly it was made up of wooden houses, of which the poorest stood on piles stretching far into the water.

Piercing cries and laughter sounded from the pier. The *Esperanza* detached itself from the tangle of boats. Towing another boat she slowly moved down the river. A freighter carrying logs approached, and a small canoe with a three-cornered sail was crossing the wide water.

Roberto sighed. Life at Buenaventura was conducted largely on the water. Without a boat one felt as comfortable as a fish on land, which is precisely how Roberto felt. Two weeks ago his boat, of which he was so proud, had been rammed. It must have happened in the night while it was moored to the landing stage. Of course, no one knew how it had happened, no one had noticed anything, and no one had been able to tell him how he could get another boat.

One thing is certain. I need not ask my father, Roberto thought gloomily. In a few days the holidays would start, and Roberto would get his report card. He did not believe his marks would inspire his father to reward him with a new boat.

As if it wasn't bad enough that his boat had been wrecked, the outboard motor had been attached to it, because he had forgotten to carry it home in the car that evening. He had managed to dig it out of the mud the next day, but the accident had not done the motor much good.

Roberto heard a noise. Looking back, he saw the old

Negro with the grizzled hair clattering down the staircase. Roberto debated whether or not to leave too, but he had gone to the factory in the hope of finding the boats of old Josué. For on one of those boats was Ordulio.

Ordulio tended the engines, and he knew everything there was to know about motors. Roberto wanted to ask Ordulio to help him fix the outboard motor, which at present lay dismantled on the floor of his father's garage. So Roberto remained alone in the silent attic, among the hanging nets, and stared across the water.

Only toward the end of the afternoon was his patience rewarded. He saw three little fishing boats circling the mangrove island and sailing up the river. They were the *Villeta,* the *Buga,* and the *Pereira.* Ordulio would be on the first one, the *Villeta.*

Roberto's father did business with about thirty boats, which brought him shrimps to process. These boats were the property of various shipowners; Gomez was one of them. They equipped the boats and paid the captains according to the catch. But with old Josué things were a little different. He had started as a general helper on a dirty old freighter. He had sailed all his life and knew the sea from Panama to Chile as no one else did. Now he was proprietor of three boats and still sailed as captain on the first one he had bought, the *Villeta.* Old Josué was not only a practiced sailor, he was an excellent shrimp fisherman. He had brought home good catches for years to Roberto's father. His elder sons, Julio and

Alfonso, were captains on the *Buga* and the *Pereira*. The two younger brothers, Enrique and Augusto, sailed with their father on the *Villeta,* where Ordulio was now the engineer.

Ordulio had turned up a few months ago in Buenaventura. No one knew exactly where he had come from, but Roberto had liked him immediately. After the accident to his boat, Ordulio had been the only one to show him some compassion. Old Josué had told Roberto to be more careful of his possessions; the four brothers made some feeble remarks and then ignored Roberto. Only Ordulio had listened patiently to him and advised him to dismantle the motor and clean it.

Roberto left his watching post, bounded down the attic steps, and ran out on the pier.

Faultlessly old Josué tacked his boat between the other boats to the landing stage. The *Buga* and the *Pereira* followed alongside and moored next to it. Hawsers were thrown and caught. Enrique and Augusto stood on deck in underpants. Their muscular torsos gleamed with sweat. The *Buga* and the *Pereira* had a Japanese crew. These men were expert sailors, and though they did not know a word of Spanish, they understood what was expected of them. The large muscular blacks serving on most of the boats paid no attention to the thin, dried-up men, who usually clustered together silently. Now too they formed a huddle.

Through the open doors of the cabin Roberto saw old Josué, dressing before leaving the boat. He pulled up his trousers, donned his Panama hat, and picked up his shoes in his hand. Barefoot he walked across the deck, and then, surprisingly quickly for an old man, he swung down to the landing stage. There he put on his shoes and slowly knotted the laces.

"Ola, Josué," called Roberto. "Have a good catch?"

"It could have been better," grumbled Josué, without looking up. He could permit himself this lack of enthusiasm. Everyone knew what an excellent fisherman he was.

"So, landlubber, how are you? Have you found another boat yet?" Roberto turned and looked into the broad, not too intelligent face of Augusto.

"No. How would I get one so soon?" answered Roberto.

"You should try Ling Pa's," Julio called from his boat. Roberto looked at him in astonishment. Ling Pa was a Chinese who sold the most varied articles, from food to ship's necessities, in his warehouse in town. But Roberto had never heard that he dealt in boats.

"Ling Pa?" he repeated stupidly. "What would I do there?"

"Ask him if he has an old tomato crate for you," shouted Julio.

Everybody began to laugh, and Julio himself laughed the loudest. Only the Japanese crew did not join in. They sat staring about them with expressionless faces.

Though he had heard the remark, old Josué did not laugh either. He turned to his oldest son and asked, "Well, what's keeping you?" The question sounded like an order. The captains of the *Buga* and the *Pereira,* both young, strong fellows, climbed meekly down and followed the old, sinewy man to the factory.

Roberto watched them go with satisfaction.

Old Josué wasn't a bad fellow. He was dour and taciturn, but that was his nature. He was certainly worth more than all his four sons together. If Josué hadn't been their father, Julio and Alfonso would not be captains. They sailed in the wake of their father. They came and went behind the *Villeta.* The only knowledge they had of the sea was that it was wet.

Ordulio, the engineer, had come out of the hot engine room. Slowly he wiped his broad dirty torso and his muscular arms with a dirty towel.

Roberto brightened when he saw him. "Ha, Ordulio!" he called. "I've been waiting for you all afternoon!"

"For me?" said Ordulio, as if he thought it strange that anyone should wait for him.

"Yes, for you. Do you remember that you told me to clean my outboard motor? Now I've taken it apart, and it is lying on the floor of our garage."

Ordulio burst out laughing. His teeth glittered in his broad, brown face. One could see that Ordulio did not come from the coast. His short, broad build and high cheekbones betrayed the strong Indian strain from the highlands. "That's not too good," he said. "And what about your boat?"

"Oh, I can forget about it," Roberto answered gloomily.

Old Josué, with Alfonso behind him, was coming back. "Come on, boys. Let's start," he commanded.

"We'll see each other later," Ordulio said, before he turned away.

He opened the trapdoor with Enrique, revealing the four great tanks in the hold. With shovels they dug out the shrimps from under the slivers of ice and into wire baskets. Augusto and Julio lifted the baskets from the landing stage. Then they carried them, dripping, from the pier to the scales.

"Make way, make way," they called out.

Roberto thought about going home. Ordulio had no time for him, and it began to rain suddenly. For a quarter of an hour the water poured down; then it stopped.

Roberto sauntered from the factory to the town. Men were drinking in front of the dilapidated bars and shanties along the side of the road. Women chatted and children played on the wooden slats above the silt strip. Soon Roberto arrived at the bridge that connected the island on which the town was built with the mainland. Though usually full of traffic, it held only one other pedestrian at that moment. A man in a colorful shirt, he was already halfway across.

He must be a stranger, thought Roberto. No one walked so quickly in Buenaventura. Probably he was a passenger of some ship, and he was worried that it would leave without him. Roberto grinned as he followed the man.

The stranger had almost reached the end of the bridge. He was suffering from the heat, for he pulled out his handkerchief and mopped his face. Roberto saw something fall from the man's pocket to the ground.

"Hey," cried Roberto. "Hey, you've lost something!" But the stranger did not hear him. He looked neither up nor down and hurried on.

Roberto walked to the dark object on the bridge deck and bent to pick it up. "He's lost his wallet!" he exclaimed.

The wallet was made of supple dark leather. Roberto looked at it from all sides before he opened it. His eyes widened with astonishment when he observed its contents. Never had he seen so much money—all dollar bills, no pesos.

Dazed, Roberto contemplated the fat wallet in his hand. The tooting of a truck brought him to his senses. He looked for the stranger, but the man was nowhere to be seen.

Roberto began to run, in the hope of overtaking him. He ran to the harbor and searched along the quay. There was no seafaring ship there. He ran to the big hotel on the bay. But nowhere did he see a man in a colorful shirt. Clutching the wallet in his pocket, he searched further in the little park by the water and in the narrow shopping streets. He peered into all the little shops and bars.

At last he came to the warehouse of Ling Pa. You could not call Ling Pa's place of business a shop. It was an enormous dark building whose double doors stood wide open in the daytime. Soft-drink bottles, stacks of gray underwear, and cakes of soap were piled up in motley confusion. Scattered all around were balls of string, barrels of tar, and pots of paint. Ship lanterns and fishing nets hung from the ceiling. At the rear of the warehouse was a storage place of potatoes, beans, rice, and cornstarch. The bags and bales were stacked up to the ceiling, with narrow aisles in between. It was a dark, dusty labyrinth with a musty smell.

Above the storage place, on a platform one could reach only by a rickety ladder, Ling Pa reigned behind his desk. Ling Pa was a cunning businessman with sharp, beady eyes. He sat huddled on his platform like an eagle on his aerie, and nothing escaped him. He knew exactly who came into his store and who passed by. He knew gossip about the whole town.

Yes, Ling Pa knew a lot, more than he showed. He, if anyone, knew the meaning of the adage: speech is silver and silence is gold. Clearly Ling Pa liked gold better than silver.

Having noticed Roberto before he entered the store, he bent over the wooden partition of his platform. "Are you looking for something?" he asked. Roberto looked up, startled, into Ling Pa's stolid face.

"Yes . . . no. That is to say, I'm looking for someone," said Roberto, flustered.

"Oh, and who are you looking for?" drawled Ling Pa.

"I am looking for . . . a man" Roberto answered unwillingly.

"Oh, and why do you look for him here? Who is he, and what do you want with him?"

"It doesn't matter. Nothing in particular," Roberto answered evasively. He'd rather bite off his tongue than tell Ling Pa about the wallet.

Ling Pa questioned him no further but kept looking at Roberto, who felt more and more uncomfortable. He felt as if Ling Pa's sharp eyes could see through his pocket. Then he caught sight of the man in the colorful shirt, who was looking at a collection of painted coconut shells, the kind tourists liked. He seemed so relaxed that Roberto felt sure he had not yet discovered his loss.

Roberto sauntered on through the warehouse. It's a nuisance. If I speak to that man, Ling Pa will see everything, he thought with irritation. He glanced up, but Ling Pa had already withdrawn and was sitting motionless behind his desk. His eyes were closed. He looked like a sleeping bird.

Roberto slid behind a few customers and stood beside the stranger in the colorful shirt. Without turning his head, he muttered, "Please, sir, follow me outside the store."

The man beside him looked up. "What's that?" he said.

"Sh, not so loud. You must follow me outside. I have something important for you." The man inspected Roberto suspiciously. "But. . . ."

"No, not here. It is really important. Follow me quick!" Roberto turned and went out of the warehouse.

The man in the colorful sport shirt followed slowly.

No one in the warehouse had seen the exchange except Ling Pa.

Once outside, Roberto entered the dirty alley that ran beside the warehouse. Behind Ling Pa's wooden building the alley widened. There was a vacant lot there with a view of the little park and the wide bay of Buenaventura. Ling Pa had bought this lot several years before for practically nothing from a poor wretch. It had increased in value ten times since, but Ling Pa did not sell it nor did he build on it. For from his platform, high in the rear of his shop, he now had an excellent view of the wide bay where ships came and went.

Roberto looked over his shoulder. Yes, the man was following. On the empty lot, which for years had been called Ling Pa's little lot, he stopped.

With a few strides the stranger joined him. He grabbed Roberto's wrist. "Out with it, youngster. What's the meaning of all this?" he said in a menacing voice. "What important message do you think you have for me?"

Roberto was suddenly afraid. "I . . . I haven't got a m . . . message," he stammered. "I. . . I just wanted to re . . . return your w . . . wallet."

"What?"

With his free hand, Roberto hastily produced the wallet and handed it over.

The man let Roberto go and took the wallet. "Yes, that's mine," he said, astonished. "But . . . how. . . ."

"I walked behind you on the bridge and saw you lose

it," said Roberto. "I called you, but you didn't seem to hear me. I searched for you all over town."

The stranger began to chuckle. "And for your pains I scared you to death," he said. "Please, forgive me. I thought you were fooling me. I'm very grateful, of course. Here. Take this." He pressed a bill into Roberto's hand, patted him on the shoulder, and walked off across Ling Pa's vacant lot, disappearing into the park.

Roberto remained standing, dazed, the bill in his hand. He looked at it, his eyes rounding with astonishment. Fifty dollars! All of fifty dollars! Never had he had so much money! Enough for a boat!

His fist clenched around the bill, he ran home as if the devil were chasing him.

On his platform, at the rear of his warehouse, Ling Pa wiped his forehead a few times with a big white handkerchief. The partition of rough planks was always dusty.

"Interesting," muttered Ling Pa to himself. "Very interesting."

2
FELIPE'S STORY

Early morning dawn partly hid the western chain of the Andes. The mountains were wrapped in a blue haze, but above the highest peaks the sky was turning pink.

Somewhere a cock crowed, and a freighter in the bay whistled. Roberto awoke, yawned, and stretched. He heard Emperatriz moving about in the backyard. Emperatriz was the black cook who ruled over Roberto's home. She had an imposing appearance: large and broad with muscular arms, broad, bony hands, and broad flat feet. Her gleaming black hair, stiff as wire, stood up on her head in countless braided plaits. She was very proud of this hairdo and spent much time and effort on it. To Roberto's father's irritation and to his mother's despair, she interfered with everything.

Roberto listened to the sounds of the slowly awakening town. Near the harbor, behind the house, trucks tooted and a dog barked. Roberto raised himself; he had heard another sound. Someone was softly rattling the big entrance gate to the yard.

A voice whispered, "Emperatriz. Hey, pst! Emperatriz!"

Roberto slid out of bed and peered through the shutters. In the gray morning light he saw a big muscular black man standing before the gate. "It is Aníbal," he muttered. "What luck! Just when I need him!"

In the yard approaching footsteps sounded. Emperatriz, barefooted, came slowly, unhurried. "So it's you," she said to her brother. The lock creaked. Aníbal pushed open the gate and slipped inside.

Roberto wanted to run immediately to meet him, but he thought it would be wiser to take his shower first before the water in the tank on the roof had been used by Emperatriz or the laundress for other purposes. Buenaventura had a water shortage. In the middle of the day, at its hottest, there was no water in the pipes at all. If it did not rain for a few days, which seldom happened, everyone complained loudly.

Roberto showered, put on his clothes, and ran into the yard. At the threshold of the ironing shed sat Aníbal. He sprawled with widespread legs, his elbows on his knees, and sipped slowly at a cup of black coffee.

Emperatriz was in the kitchen, baking the corn cakes called *arepas.*

"Good morning, Aníbal. How are you?"

"*Ola,* Roberto, and how are you?"

Roberto sat down next to Aníbal. In a cage against the back wall of the garage a few brightly colored birds fluttered back and forth, twittering.

"What are they?" asked Aníbal, looking at the cage.

"Carpinteros."

"Have you had them long?"

"No. I just got them."

"You should feed them papayas," said Aníbal, smacking his lips.

"That is all you can think of—eating," said Emperatriz. She had come out of the kitchen with warm corn cakes and frowned at her brother. "That's all you come here for."

Aníbal's face split in a grin. He accepted the corn cakes. "Ah," he said. "You won't be sorry that you look after me, sister. In a short time—" He bit greedily into an *arepa.*

"Olala!" Emperatriz's lips curled disdainfully. "If I have to wait till you start working!"

Aníbal cast up his eyes. The pupils rolled up until only the white showed.

"Working? Who talks about working?" he said with his mouth full.

Emperatriz indignantly turned her back on him, and Aníbal bit with gusto into his second *arepa*.

"Aníbal, you hear things. Have you any idea how much a boat costs?" asked Roberto, when Emperatriz had vanished into the kitchen.

"A boat?" muttered Aníbal. "Who can say? They come dear at present."

"It need not be a new one," Roberto said hastily.

Aníbal chewed silently. At last he asked, "What would you give for one?"

But Roberto felt that naming a price himself would be unwise. "I just wanted to know," he said vaguely. Quickly he asked, "What do you do nowadays?"

"Oh, about everything," Aníbal answered.

"Do you still fish in Málaga Bay?" Málaga Bay was a deeply curved bay north of Buenaventura. Roberto had heard that Aníbal often went there.

Aníbal gave Roberto a sideways glance. "What makes you ask that?" he asked.

"Nothing. I was just guessing."

"I'm not fishing at present," said Aníbal. "And they won't see me soon again in Málaga Bay."

"Why not?"

"The last time I was there two whales entered the bay with me, one at either side of my canoe."

"Go on," said Roberto. "Whales!"

"You may skin me if it isn't true," said Aníbal. "Two whales."

"What happened?"

"Nothing. I was scared stiff. A creature like that needs only to wiggle its tail, and you and your canoe have had it."

"What did you do?" asked Roberto, intrigued now.

"I did nothing," said Aníbal. "I sat still as a mouse in my canoe."

"Didn't you try to get ashore?"

"No, if I'd done that, they'd have been sure to notice me. I just sat motionless until they were gone. But I can tell you that there have been moments in my life I've enjoyed more."

"I can imagine," said Roberto. He did not know what to think of Aníbal's story.

Emperatriz appeared at the open door of the kitchen. "Please come to breakfast, Roberto," she called. "It's been ready for some time, and I don't want to have it to clean up after the visitors arrive."

Roberto jumped up. "Visitors! Are there going to be visitors? Who's coming?" he asked eagerly.

"Don Luís phoned from Cali yesterday. He will be here soon."

"And Felipe?" Roberto asked. "Is he coming too?"

"Who knows?" said Emperatriz, turning away.

When Roberto had lived in Cali, Felipe and he had been inseparable friends. And though Roberto had been in Buenaventura for many years now, the friendship had lasted. Felipe's parents had a vacation home at La Bocana, the coastal region at the mouth of Buenaventura Bay, and they went there every vacation with their family. Roberto always joined them so that the boys still saw each other several times a year.

Roberto paced back and forth all morning, impatiently awaiting the visitors. At last a car stopped before the gate. When Roberto rushed out, Felipe was already jumping out of the car.

"There you are. I've been waiting all morning for you!" shouted Roberto.

"Did you know we were coming? We couldn't make any better time. The road was in bad shape. I was afraid you wouldn't be home," Felipe rattled off in one breath.

"Come on." Roberto impatiently pulled Felipe's arm.

Don Pablo, Roberto's father, and Doña María, Roberto's mother, went to sit on the front porch with Don Luís. Emperatriz came with coffee, and the two boys went to Roberto's room.

"When Father came home yesterday and said he had to go to Buenaventura, I asked if I could go too since it was Saturday," said Felipe. "So here I am." He looked around with admiration at Roberto's cosy room, full of his treasures.

"What happened to your stuffed tortoise?" he asked.

"I had to throw it out. It started to stink," answered Roberto.

"That's a shame." Felipe took up the sword of a swordfish, turning it around in his hands. "How did you get hold of this?"

"A shrimp fisherman gave it to me."

"You're lucky!"

"Yes, but the biggest piece of luck happened yesterday." Roberto showed his friend the fifty-dollar bill.

"Who gave you *that?*" asked Felipe, amazed.

Roberto told him the whole story.

"Go on. It's incredible," said Felipe. "Did he give it to you just like that?"

"Yes, after he first almost broke my arm."

"Oh, you've got to suffer a little for something like that," said Felipe callously. "Was he an American? What language did he speak?"

"Ordinary Spanish. I thought at first that he was a foreigner too."

"What are you going to do with the money?"

"I want to buy a new boat. You know they wrecked my boat in a collision? But this morning Aníbal, Emperatriz's brother, said boats were very expensive now."

"Perhaps you can make one yourself. If you only have to buy the wood, it will be cheaper," said Felipe practically.

"That's a good idea. Perhaps we can work at it together during vacation."

Felipe's face fell. "We may not go to La Bocana this vacation," he answered.

Roberto was dismayed. "Why not?" he asked.

"Because. . . . " Felipe hesitated a moment. "Can you keep a secret?"

"Of course," said Roberto readily.

"Well, you know that there's a lot of smuggling in Buenaventura."

Roberto grinned a bit scornfully. "You're telling me," he said.

"Yes, but what's happening now is much worse than just plain smuggling."

"What's happening then?"

"They are smuggling in weapons on a large scale."

"Weapons?" repeated Roberto. Now he was all ears.

"Yes, weapons. That's much worse than smuggling cigarettes and whiskey and that sort of thing."

Roberto nodded. "How did they find out?" he asked.

"They came across a cache of weapons in the mountains near Bogotá. Revolvers and machine guns. And a few days later they discovered a car full of hand grenades on the way to Cali."

"On the way to Cali!" exclaimed Roberto. His face expressed regret that he had missed such an event.

"Yes, on the way to Cali. At the customs, where the cars going inland from Buenaventura are inspected."

"That takes nerve. To drive past the customs with a car full of smuggled hand grenades!" said Roberto.

"Yes, and the driver of the car said coolly that he was on his way to the airport. As you know, they don't search cars going to the airport."

Roberto nodded. "That was pretty cool. And then what happened?"

"The customs officers must have had special orders, because the trick didn't work. The driver had to get out and let his car be searched."

"And then?"

"The driver vanished at once into the underbrush. A moment later the officers found the hand grenades. They learned later that the car had been stolen, so it didn't help them much."

Roberto whistled between his teeth. "Too bad," he said. "But I don't understand what it has to do with your vacation."

"I'll tell you," said Felipe. "The government has taken an interest in the business, because they feel that there's something behind all this." Felipe looked significantly at Roberto.

"You mean, they're afraid of a revolution," said Roberto.

Felipe nodded. "Exactly," he said.

"But what has all that to do with *you*?" Roberto asked again. "Why can't you have your vacation?"

"Because the government has given my father instructions to take care of this matter," said Felipe importantly. "And my mother says that she has no intention of going alone with us to La Bocana while my father is looking for a bunch of weapons smugglers."

"Oh," said Roberto, baffled. A moment later he added, "But if your father has to be in Buenaventura, it would be better if you went to your vacation house. Then he won't have to drive to Cali all the time."

"Yes, that's what Father and I think. But my mother disagrees. She says my father may have to go out in the middle of the night, and then she'd be left alone."

"So we're stuck," said Roberto. He stood before his window, which looked out on the garden and the road with its border of palms. It was gloomy weather. The fronds of the palms rustled.

"Is it raining?" asked Felipe.

"Just beginning to," answered Roberto. The first heavy drops started to fall. A moment later it was pouring. The boys heard the men on the porch shoving their chairs inside.

"Remember, don't repeat any of what I told you to your father," warned Felipe.

"Why not?"

"Father doesn't want it talked about. It only makes his work more difficult, he says."

"It will be known soon enough. Everyone always knows everything in Buenaventura."

"Yes, but still. . . ."

"Oh, don't worry. I'll be as silent as a priest," promised Roberto.

Don Luís stuck his head around the corner of the door. "It's time to go, Felipe," he said.

"But it's raining!" both boys exclaimed simultaneously.

"You won't melt. The car is in the front of the gate," answered Don Luís. His head disappeared. The boys went to the living room. It began to rain so hard that they could hardly see the houses opposite.

"You'd better wait a bit, Luís," said Doña María. "You'll be drenched before you get into the car."

They stood in front of the open doors of the living room and looked at the streaming rain. In the garden great pools were forming, and the water flowed like a river over the concrete road.

"Such weather!" said Don Luís.

"Well, we're known to have the heaviest rainfall in the world," said Don Pablo. "Three hundred and fifty inches of rain a year is no joke."

They kept on watching the rain. Emperatriz entered with more coffee. At last the weather cleared. Don Luís and Felipe hurried to the car.

"Try and make her see it your way!" Roberto called after his friend.

"I will," Felipe called back.

The car started. Felipe hung out a window and waved till the car rounded a corner. While driving through the mountains to Cali, Felipe resolved to try to persuade his mother to go to La Bocana after all.

3

A WALK THROUGH VENICE

"It's a fine state of affairs," said Don Pablo, entering the porch. He sat down heavily in a chair and rubbed his forehead. His face looked grave.

"What happened?" Doña María and Roberto asked at the same time.

"César Gomez has lost two of his boats."

Doña María threw her husband a startled glance.

Roberto cried out, "It isn't possible."

"It's a strange story," said Don Pablo.

"What happened?" asked Doña María again.

"Gomez sent two of his boats to Panama. One had to be repaired, and it was towed by the other. When they were at sea, the oil pipes of the towing boat burst, the fuel ran out, and they drifted."

"Couldn't they ask for help? They have a radio on board," said Roberto.

"They probably tried, but their radio isn't very strong. In any case, a Norwegian ship passed, and they asked it for help. They had repaired the pipes somewhat, but they needed fuel, and the Norwegians said they had no time to supply them with it."

"But they *have* to help!" cried Roberto, scandalized.

Don Pablo shrugged his shoulders. "Those poor fellows on the fishing boats could not force them to, could they?" he said.

"Poor people," said Doña María compassionately.

"The crew of the fishing boats then boarded the Norwegian, leaving one man with the boats."

"No!" cried Roberto.

Don Pablo nodded. "Yes," he said. "It's difficult to believe, but that's what they did. The men told it all when they arrived with the Norwegian ship in Panama. Gomez got the story there."

"What happened then?" asked Roberto.

"The two boats disappeared. They've been searching for them with an airplane, but they can't be found."

"And that one man?" asked Roberto.

"He probably went down with the boats," said Don Pablo.

"Who was it?"

His father shrugged his shoulders, and Roberto thought involuntarily of Magdaleno, who had gone with those boats to Panama.

"What does Gomez say about it?" asked Doña María.

"Gomez is furious," said Don Pablo. "He calls it a scandal. He was at the factory this morning, and there was no reasoning with him. All he could talk about was his boats."

Emperatriz entered with three cups of black coffee. She caught Don Pablo's last words. "Ah," she said. "Did the *señor* hear about it? César Gomez has lost two of his boats at sea, or so he says."

Don Pablo stirred his coffee silently, but Doña María said, "Come, come, Emperatriz. If Señor Gomez says so, it must be true. It's a terrible loss for the poor man."

Emperatriz gave a disdainful sniff. "César Gomez can say what he likes. His father was no good either. Everyone in Buenaventura knows how he got rich. Easy come, easy go. That's what I say." She went back to the kitchen. Her bare feet slapped softly on the tiles. The kitchen door slammed shut.

"What was the matter with Gomez's father?" Roberto asked immediately.

Don Pablo rose. "I have to be off," he said.

"Mother, do you know what Emperatriz meant?" asked Roberto again, when his father had left.

"Oh, people gossip so," said Doña María evasively. Quickly she added, "Have you heard from Felipe? When is he coming?"

Roberto's face darkened. "He may not come at all," he said. "His mother doesn't want to go to La Bocana this vacation."

"Oh yes, that's true," said Doña María. "I can't say that I blame her!"

"Did you hear about it?" asked Roberto.

Doña María nodded. "It's a terrible situation," she said. "Who knows how many weapons have already been smuggled into the country . . . and for what purpose? It's criminal!"

"Would the smugglers know why the weapons are brought into the country?"

"They wouldn't care. People who do that sort of thing think only of the money. They are dangerous criminals who'll stop at nothing." There was a moment's silence, then Doña María added thoughtfully, "I can well imagine that Felipe's mother doesn't care to come with the children to La Bocana. It's so lonely there along the coast, at the edge of the jungle."

"But there's a whole row of fishermen's huts, and on Sunday visitors come from town," objected Roberto.

"Yes, all right. But something bad could happen at a time like this."

"I think it's awful not to see Felipe for a whole vacation."

Doña María smiled. "I understand," she said. "How would you like to invite Felipe to come and stay with us for a while? Then you'd be together."

Roberto jumped up and ran to his mother. "Mother, that's a wonderful, marvelous idea," he shouted.

Doña María warded him off hastily. "Watch out. You're hugging me too hard."

Roberto let his mother go. "I'll spare you, because you're the only mother I have," he said condescendingly.

Doña María laughed. "Thanks for the compliment," she said. "And now you'd better find something to do. Have you no homework?"

"No, the day after tomorrow the holidays start," answered Roberto. "I'm going to call Felipe at once, and then I'll go to the factory."

Near the factory there was the usual bustle. Women and girls in garish dresses stood cleaning shrimp. Boats came tacking into the landing stage. Shrimps were unloaded and weighed.

The *Villeta,* the *Buga,* and the *Pereira* had all been made ready for departure.

The day before the parcels with food from Ling Pa had been brought on board. Now the *Villeta* was being filled with fuel, and the last baskets of ice were poured into the tanks under the deck.

Roberto looked around. He didn't see Ordulio anywhere, but Enrique and Augusto stood on the pier.

"Ola, Roberto. Have you heard about Gomez?" Enrique cried at once.

Roberto nodded.

"He's terribly upset, just the way you were about your boat." Enrique grinned, and the small eyes in his broad face glittered with malice. "Have you got another boat yet?"

"Not yet. I haven't decided whether I'll buy one or build one," said Roberto loftily.

The two brothers looked at Roberto in amazement. After a pause Enrique said hesitatingly, "New boats are expensive nowadays."

Roberto pretended not to notice their surprise. "Well," he said cheerfuly, "then I'll have to get the wood and build one myself."

"What's that, Roberto? Are you going to build a boat?" came Ordulio's voice. He had just come on board and had caught Roberto's last words.

"Yes, if I can get cheap wood. Otherwise, it won't be worthwhile," said Roberto.

"Then you must go to the sawmill on the coast," advised Ordulio. "If you fetch the wood yourself in a canoe, you can get it a lot more cheaply."

"I can see Roberto paddling a canoe along the coast," sneered Augusto. "He wouldn't be able to manage it. I'd just as soon buy that old wreck of a boat that's lying on Manuel el Bobo's banana plantation."

"Is there a boat there?" asked Roberto, interested.

Old Josué appeared on deck. He looked around him,

and his commanding eye fell on the group on the pier.

"What the devil! Have you nothing to do but to stand babbling?" he shouted angrily.

Enrique and Augusto hastily grabbed their empty ice baskets and ran off. Ordulio dove into the engine room. Old Josué spat disdainfully into the water and re-entered the cabin.

Roberto sat down on the pier. It was low tide. On the broad strip of mud under the factory a few black boys were searching for shrimps. There was a lot of refuse there, and the pilings on which the factory rested were slimy and green.

Ordulio reappeared on deck. Roberto had hoped to speak to him again. "Hey, Ordulio!" he called. "Couldn't you help me with my outboard motor?"

"Haven't you fixed it yet?" asked Ordulio with interest. "Why not?"

"I tried, but I can't put it together," said Roberto. "I wish you would take a look at it."

"Of course, I'll look at it for you, but you'll have to wait till we put in again."

"All right," said Roberto. "As soon as you're in, I'll be here."

Ordulio laughed. "Fine," he said. "But now I have to get back to work. See you later, Roberto!"

"See you later, Ordulio, and have a good trip!" He saw Ordulio go into the engine room. He waved and Ordulio waved back. Then his head disappeared.

Roberto got up and left. Passing his father's office, he

heard the excited voice of Gomez, who was discussing his boats and verbally abusing the captain and the crew of the Norwegian ship. The man who had gone down with the boats was not even mentioned.

Roberto left the factory and went back to town. He remembered the words of Emperatriz: "Easy come, easy go," she had said. What could she have meant by that?

Why had Gomez's father been no good? What had he done? How had he become rich? When Emperatriz made dark insinuations and his mother would not explain them, he was sure that something must have happened. Perhaps Aníbal knew about it.

I'll walk past Aníbal's house, thought Roberto. I can ask him if he'll let me go with him in his canoe to the sawmill on the coast, and I can also ask him about Gomez.

The sun hung like a fiery disk above the darkening jungle. The day was sliding toward its end. Roberto quickened his steps. Where Aníbal lived, it was better to go by daylight.

The pile dwellings in which the greater part of the black population lived were built far out over the water. They were made out of planks and flattened tin cans. This area bore the lofty name of Venice. At high tide the water gurgled up, almost touching the floors of the huts. At low tide, as it was now, one could see the muddy silt strip through the holes and splits in the planks. It was rapidly getting darker. Roberto picked his way carefully over the rickety plank bridges between the hovels. One plank bent with a squeal under his weight; a pole rolled away from under his foot. Hastily he jumped onto something firmer.

Dance music blared from the huts. Somewhere a woman shrieked; a man swore. Half-naked childen played on the rotting plank bridge above the musty silt strip where pools of water had been left by the tide.

On a crossing point of several bridges, connected by one swaying plank, Roberto stood still and looked around. He knew that Aníbal lived in Venice, but he did not know exactly where. A skinny woman approached. She had a small cigar in her mouth and carried a wooden box filled with fish on her head. Her gait was supple and sure; her broad feet carried her unerringly over the narrow plank.

"Good evening. Can you tell me where Aníbal lives?" asked Roberto. The woman muttered something unintelligible and vanished in the shadows between the huts. Roberto walked on haphazardly. A naked urchin was relieving himself through a break in the plank walk. A little child and a big dog ate rice together out of the same bowl. A little farther on a group of men sat together, gossiping, drinking, and laughing.

Roberto stopped beside them. "I'm looking for Aníbal," he said. "Do you know where he lives?"

"Whom do you want?"

"Aníbal."

One of the men pointed to the end of the alley. "There, in that hut, the next to last one before you come to the water again."

Roberto thanked them and walked to the place he had indicated. He saw a canoe lying under the hut. Good, Aníbal is home, he thought. The door was shut but through the cracks came a faint streak of light. He heard subdued talk inside the hut.

"Hey, Aníbal, are you there? It's me, Roberto!"

The talk died. The door opened, and Aníbal appeared. He leaned against the doorframe and let the door fall shut against his shoulder. He had a half-empty beer bottle in his hand. "*Ola,* Roberto," he said. "How did you happen to come this way?"

"I came to visit you."

"Me? Why?"

"No reason," Roberto said vaguely. He did not feel this reception was encouraging enough to start talking about Gomez's father.

"Ah!" said Aníbal. There was a moment's silence.

Roberto felt strongly that he wasn't welcome. "When . . . when are you coming to visit us again?" he asked, to say something.

Aníbal shrugged his shoulders. "Who knows?"

"I . . . I came to ask if you would take me with you sometime when you go out along the coast in your canoe."

"Along the coast? Why?"

"I want to buy wood to build a boat. I want to make it myself."

"Ah, good. I'll come by soon. Then we'll talk about it." Aníbal put the beer bottle to his mouth and emptied it in one draught.

"Well, I'll be going then."

"All right. So long. You'll see me presently," said Aníbal once more.

Roberto went back over the uneven bridges full of gaping holes. As he shuffled cautiously over some shaky bamboo poles someone threw a pan of dirty water out of the open door of a hut. It barely missed him.

"Hey, look out!" Roberto cried, startled.

"And what do *you* want?" asked a lanky fellow aggressively from the doorway. Immediately several heads appeared behind him. It seemed impossible that a little hut could harbor so many people.

The boy stepped on the plank bridge barring Roberto's way menacingly. The other children pushed out behind him. Like a black cluster they confronted Roberto.

"Let me through," said Roberto. The big boy didn't answer. He looked at Roberto with animosity and made no move to get out of the way. Roberto smelled liquor on his breath. The smaller boys began to snicker. Roberto's hands itched, but he was sensible enough to keep them out of action. He realized that in this case he would do better to give way. Without another word he turned and walked back. A little farther he saw a narrow passage between huts. He tried to feel his way along the alley. It had become completely dark now.

Roberto heard something stir behind him. Had the

boys followed him? He turned quickly but saw nothing. As he went on, still looking back, he collided with someone.

"Look where you're going, boy," drawled a familiar voice.

"Ling Pa!" cried Roberto. "What are you doing here?"

"I'd better ask you that," said Ling Pa.

Even in the dark Roberto felt Ling Pa's eyes fixed on him. "I . . . ah . . . am on my way home," he babbled.

"Aren't you going in the wrong direction?" Ling Pa asked sarcastically.

"No . . . yes. . . . I mean, I'm going through the alley," Roberto answered unwillingly. He didn't want Ling Pa to know he had been running away.

Ling Pa's dark head moved against the lighter sky as he slowly shook his head.

"Very strange," he said. "Very, very strange." Then he went ponderously on his way. For a moment he was revealed in a ray of light, a stout Chinese in an immaculate white suit, an unusual apparition in that neighborhood.

Roberto slid into the dark alley. He picked his way between the hovels and was glad when he reached firm land without further incident. Quickly he walked through the town in the direction of his house. The shops were lit, and dance music blared from the bars. Far out in the dark bay twinkled the lights of the light buoys.

The night was oppressive; moon and stars were hidden by clouds. Darkness enveloped the little town and covered the broad rivers and endless jungle. Somewhere on a small mountain path, far in the Andes, a group of grim men were bringing new weapons farther into the country.

4

ANÍBAL CAUSES COMMOTION

The holidays had begun, and Felipe had arrived. The two boys stood in the backyard near the birdcage. The gleaming black birds with their red breasts and gray bibs hopped to and fro. Roberto fed them papaya. They pecked greedily at the big, juicy pieces of fruit.

"They like it a lot," said Felipe.

"Yes, Aníbal told me to give it to them."

"Do you see him sometimes?"

Roberto sighed. "No. A while ago he said he'd come soon. I wanted him to take me along the coast in his canoe to buy wood for my boat. But he never came."

"Perhaps he is too busy," suggested Felipe.

Roberto laughed. "Emperatriz should hear that! I don't believe she's very pleased with her brother. He's really a lazy one."

"I'd like to go along the coast in a canoe," said Felipe. "Can't we go to Aníbal and ask him?"

"There's little chance we'd find him home," said Roberto quickly. He did not have the faintest wish to go back to Venice.

"Where is he then, do you think?"

"If he isn't in his canoe in the water, he'll be hanging around in the town somewhere."

"Let's go into town then, and see if we can find him," proposed Felipe.

They walked through the gate and into the town, toward the quay. The sky was overcast, and there was a clammy, suffocating heat. The water in the bay lay smooth as a mirror. Along the far shore the jungle spread dark and green. A cargo boat entered the bay and went upstream to anchor. The boys ambled along the waterfront and through the park, crossing the small, busy town square. Everywhere on stone benches under the palms, men were talking. But Aníbal wasn't there. They did not see him anywhere.

They sauntered through the narrow shopping streets and came to Ling Pa's warehouse. As usual the Chinese sat on his platform at the rear of his store.

Felipe nudged Roberto. "There he sits, spying again," he said. "Is he rusted fast to that platform?"

"No." Roberto grinned. "A few days ago I bumped into him. You'd never guess where."

"Where?"

"In Venice!"

"In Venice? What were *you* doing there?"

"I wanted to ask Aníbal about Gomez's father, but he didn't even invite me in."

"No? That's funny. Why not?"

Roberto shrugged his shoulders. "He had a visitor. I heard them talk!"

"Perhaps he didn't want you to know who was with him," guessed Felipe.

"As if I cared what friends Aníbal has."

"What was Ling Pa's business in Venice?"

"He didn't tell me."

"Perhaps Ling Pa was the one with Aníbal," said Felipe shrewdly.

"You might have something there!" Roberto stood still in the middle of the street. "I met him close by!"

"There, you see? Perhaps he can tell us where Aníbal is now," said Felipe impetuously. "Come on. Let's ask him!" He dragged Roberto with him into the warehouse.

Ling Pa saw the boys come in and make straight for

the rickety stairs leading to his platform. He waited, motionless.

"Good afternoon, Ling Pa," said the boys.

"What can I do for you?" Ling Pa asked.

"Do you know where er . . . we can find Aníbal?" asked Roberto.

Ling Pa looked searchingly at the boys. "Aníbal," he repeated. "I know no Aníbal. Why do you want him?"

"Aníbal, who lives in Venice. He is . . . er . . . the brother of our cook, and . . . er . . . we must speak to him," stuttered Roberto.

"Oh?" said Ling Pa. "That's very interesting. I'm sorry I can't help you. My business is not an information service." He looked coldly at the boys.

Roberto and Felipe slunk away.

Once outside, Felipe said "So that's one thing we've learned. Ling Pa doesn't even know Aníbal."

"At least, that's what he says," grumbled Roberto. He wasn't sure he hadn't been teased by Ling Pa.

"What business is it of ours anyway?" Felipe continued. "Only it's too bad we don't know where to look for Aníbal now."

They sauntered through the unpaved, dusty streets, past faded wooden houses and past long rows of large trucks near the docks. They could not find Aníbal anywhere.

"A pity. I'd have liked a trip over the water," Felipe said ruefully.

"If only I had a boat." Roberto sighed. Suddenly he stopped. "That boat on Manuel el Bobo's banana plantation," he cried. "I'd forgotten about it!"

"What kind of a boat is it?" Felipe was interested.

"I don't know, but the other day Augusto told me that there is one on Manuel el Bobo's plantation."

"Who is Manuel el Bobo, and where is the plantation?" asked Felipe.

"The plantation lies outside the town, past the bridge over the Dagua. Manuel el Bobo is the overseer of the plantation. People say he's a queer fellow. He lives there with his seven sons. I believe those boys never went to school. Manuel el Bobo is almost always drunk, and the boys have to do the work. The plantation is very big and terribly neglected. It's no wonder when Manuel el Bobo is mostly on his bed, sleeping off his hangovers. He hardly ever sets foot on the plantation."

Felipe began to laugh. "A fine overseer," he praised. "If I were the owner of the plantation, I'd have fired him long ago.'

"Oh, the owner never goes there, I believe. He's a rich man and lives abroad," answered Roberto.

"Well, it isn't my headache," said Felipe. "Shall we go to the plantation tomorrow and look at the boat? I'm fed up with looking for Aníbal."

"All right we'll start early," said Roberto.

It began to rain. In a moment the dusty roads were transformed into pools of mud. The boys ran home.

When they pushed open the garden gate they saw

Don Pablo and Doña María sitting on the porch. Between them sat César Gomez. Emperatriz came in with beer and Coca-Cola.

"Bring some more beer presently," said Don Pablo to Emperatriz, before she padded off on her bare feet.

Outside the lukewarm raindrops drummed on plants and bushes. Despite the rain they all remained on the porch. It was too oppressive inside. They only pushed their chairs back a bit.

César Gomez asked the boys how things were with them and what they'd done all day. He made jokes and told stories.

Encouraged by this jovial attitude, Roberto said, "What a strange business that was with those boats of yours."

The expression on Gomez's face changed immediately. "Strange?" he repeated sharply. "Why strange?"

"Oh, nothing. I just meant what an unfortunate business," Roberto amended hastily.

"Ah, yes, if that's what you meant. Yes, it was a heavy blow. A big financial setback, I can tell you that. It's a bad time for everyone. That business about weapon smuggling. The boats are constantly being stopped and inspected."

César Gomez stroked his florid face with his little plump hand; his little sharp eyes narrowed. "Between us, I think the customs are wasting time and money. They obstruct commerce and hinder the people who are earning their bread honestly."

Don Pablo objected mildly. "The innocent always have to suffer for the guilty. I agree that the strict control takes time and is hampering. But when smugglers aren't opposed, there is still more damage. It's a case of community interest, not individual interest."

"Maybe," admitted Gomez with a short laugh. "But I think first of my own pocket."

Roberto remembered suddenly Magdaleno of the *Esperanza,* who had called Gomez a money monger. And then the words of Emperatriz came to his mind; what had she meant? What had been wrong with Gomez's father? He resolved to find out. Thoughtfully he stared at the garden. It wasn't raining anymore, but heavy drops still fell from the bushes onto the muddy ground.

A woman with a newspaper protecting her head pushed open the big gate leading to the garage. She ran across the muddy yard to the back of the house.

Don Pablo emptied his glass and César Gomez followed his example. "Go and see why Emperatriz isn't bringing us more beer," Don Pablo asked his son.

Roberto got up. At that moment loud wailings came from the direction of the kitchen.

"Heavens, what's that!" said Don Pablo.

"It's Emperatriz." Doña María looked startled. "What's happened?"

"I saw someone come into the yard," said Roberto. "A woman."

"Yes, I saw her too," agreed Felipe.

The wailing in the kitchen continued.

"I must go and see," said Doña María. She hastened to the kitchen. Roberto and Felipe ran after her.

Emperatriz sat on a chair in the middle of the kitchen. She held her head with her big hands and rocked to and fro in despair.

"Ai . . . ai . . . ai!" she whimpered.

"Emperatriz, did you fall?" asked Doña María. Emperatriz did not answer. She kept on rocking and moaning.

"What's the matter? Answer me, Emperatriz," said Doña María, raising her voice.

"Ai . . . ai . . . the shame. I'll never get over it!" wailed Emperatriz. "Madre de Dios, how is it possible!"

Don Pablo appeared in the doorway. "What's the matter?" he asked. "Are you sick? Emperatriz, answer me!"

"With your permission, *señora,"* said a strange voice.

They all looked up. Half hidden behind the outside door stood a woman. She was nervously twisting the edge of her blouse.

"Who are you?" asked Doña María.

"Catalina, at your service, *señora.* I'm a cousin of Emperatriz. The daughter of the sister of the mother of. . . ."

"Oh, the shame! My mother would have died of it!" wailed Emperatriz. "We are a decent family; we are no *tusos."* Emperatriz again grabbed her head and showed the length of her plaits. Those who could not boast the proper length of hair were called *tusos* and were considered to have less social status.

"That may be so," said Don Pablo impatiently. "But in Heaven's name, what's *happened?*"

"It's about Aníbal, *señor,*" said Catalina. "They've come to fetch him."

"Who are *they*?"

"The . . . the police, I think."

"What?" cried Roberto. "Has he been arrested?"

Catalina shook her head.

"No," she said. "They fought and Aníbal escaped. No one knows what happened. He's gone."

Emperatriz began to moan again. She sobbed with long crooning sounds.

Don Pablo and Doña María exchanged glances. "Have you something to calm her? A sedative?" whispered Don Pablo to his wife.

Doña María hurried out of the kitchen and came back with medicine and a glass of water. She forced Emperatriz to take some. Then she and Catalina took Emperatriz to her little room at the back of the yard. Don Pablo and the boys returned to the porch, where César Gomez had remained by himself. A little later Doña María rejoined them. She had made a plateful of sandwiches and put them on the table.

"Emperatriz was completely upset," she said. "Now she's lying on the bed and does nothing but lament. Catalina and several other relatives are sitting around and lamenting with her. It's enough to drive one crazy."

Outside the darkness grew. The palms in front of the house rustled. Far away the town noises sounded, and in the backyard they could hear excited voices.

Long after César Gomez had left, the family remained sitting on the porch. Now and again the big gate creaked. Some relatives and acquaintances of Emperatriz left, others entered. Everyone wanted to know what had happened and how much Emperatriz knew. Doña María finally sighed and made preparations to go to bed. The chairs and tables were taken inside. Don Pablo shut the porch doors. Roberto and Felipe went to their room.

They talked a long time about the events of that day. Till late in the evening they heard bare feet padding across the yard.

5

MANUEL EL BOBO'S BANANA PLANTATION

It was still dark when the boys awoke.

"Hey, shall we go now?" asked Roberto softly.

"Yes, go where?" asked Felipe sleepily.

"You know, we were going to Manuel el Bobo's plantation to look at that boat."

"That's true." Felipe was awake at once and shot upright in bed.

Almost soundlessly the boys rose, dressed, and slipped through the window into the garden. It had rained again in the night; everything was cool and wet. The dripping leaves of the plants and bushes brushed past them. They walked over the muddy garden path to the gate. The gravel in the backyard crunched in the darkness. They saw a figure loom in front of them. The big gate clanked open and shut. Then the shadow lost itself in the dim light of the deserted street.

"Did you see that?" whispered Roberto.

"Who was it?" Felipe whispered back.

"Emperatriz."

"What is she doing out so early?"

"I don't know. Strange, isn't it?"

"Let's go and see what she's up to."

The boys crept through the gate. As quickly and soundlessly as they could, they entered the shadowy darkness in which Emperatriz had vanished. They saw her turn into a side street. When the boys reached the corner, she was disappearing over the shoulder of a hill.

"She's going to the waterfront."

"Do you think she's going to Venice to look for Aníbal?" asked Felipe in a low voice. Roberto shrugged his shoulders. They walked on quickly. It began to grow light. Cautiously they ascended the sloping street and stood looking down at the water below.

On the shore, which was covered with grass and shrubbery, Emperatriz stood between two houses. Cautiously she descended the steep ladder to the water.

Down below on the muddy silt strip, which was still dry, stood some miserable pile dwellings with roofs of palm leaves. Crouched between wet shrubbery, Roberto and Felipe watched Emperatriz. They saw her go to one of the huts.

A man appeared in its doorway. "Ah," he said. "You came."

"They say you can bring me to the island of La Calavera," Emperatriz answered.

"Did you hear that?" Roberto whispered, appalled. "Emperatriz wants to go to La Calavera, the Death Head Isle."

"What?" breathed Felipe. "Do you think that Aníbal is there?"

But Roberto shook his head vigorously. "Salomon lives on La Calavera," he said, with awe in his voice. "Salomon is a very old Negro. He's a medicine man, a *brujo*. The people here say he is very clever; he has a remedy for everything."

"But what do you think Emperatriz . . . ?"

"Hush!" whispered Roberto impatiently. "Look, there she goes!"

The man had descended the steps in front of his hut. He pushed his canoe from the mud into a narrow channel. Emperatriz got in. Above the wide stretch of water hung the morning mist. In the gray half-light the small mangrove island could hardly be seen. The tide had turned, and water was slowly flowing into the bay. Scarcely noticeably, the mud strip became inundated.

The man paddled the canoe over the water with powerful strokes. In the front of the narrow vessel sat Emperatriz. She sat straight up, staring fixedly at the little island that loomed before her out of the mist. La Calavera, the Death Head Isle!

The boys on shore watched her till she was swallowed up in the mist. Roberto wiped his mouth with the back of his hand. "I wish I knew what Emperatriz wanted to get from the medicine man," he said.

"Perhaps she got ill from the shock," suggested Felipe.

Roberto kept silent. He stared over the water. The mist was dissolving. In the distance lay La Calavera, the Death Head Isle. There was no sign of the canoe anymore.

"Let's go," said Felipe, "or it will get too late." The boys walked in the direction of the long, concrete bridge.

"We must try and get a ride on a truck," said Roberto. "It's too far to walk."

It was quite light by now, and it began to get warm. They were lucky. Before they came to the bridge, a truck overtook them. The boys raised their hands, and the driver stopped.

"Get in. Where are you going?"

"To Manuel el Bobo's plantation," answered Roberto. The driver nodded. They went along the highway to Cali. It was a narrow road, full of curves, right through the jungle. At the customs post they had to stop for inspection; then they went on.

When they crossed the bridge over the Dagua River, Roberto said, "It's around here somewhere." The driver stopped, the boys thanked him, and got out.

Felipe looked around. "Where is the plantation?" he said.

"I don't know exactly. I've never been there," said Roberto. "Let's follow the road for a bit."

The truck was long gone. The road was deserted. Motionless, the jungle stretched out on either side. At last they saw a path at the right side of the road. They decided to take it. The jungle that had stood there years ago had been burned down. Now it was a banana plantation.

"You see, here it is,' said Roberto happily. Felipe nodded and looked around. The path was narrow and badly kept; it showed deep wheel ruts. High banana plants towered on either side. It was very still.

"Let's go on," said Roberto impatiently.

The boys went farther into the plantation. The path curved and meandered between the banana plants, rising and falling with the hilly terrain.

"How quiet it is here," whispered Felipe. "Where would the house be?"

"Farther on, I think," said Roberto. Silently they walked some more. The torn leaves of the banana plants hung motionless over the narrow path. There wasn't a living being in sight anywhere.

"Do you really think this is it?" asked Felipe after a while. "I don't see anyone."

"It's a banana plantation at any rate. Let's go on," said Roberto optimistically.

Again the path curved, and then it widened. The boys stood in a huge bare yard. The plantation around the yard was edged by thick, dark jungle. The light green of the broad banana leaves contrasted sharply with the background of high forest trees. In the yard stood a dilapidated old house. The porch had sunk, the gate had no paint left on it, the roof showed big holes, broken tiles lay on the ground. There was no one to be seen.

Roberto and Felipe walked slowly around the house. The shutters were all closed; they hung crookedly in front of the windows. At the back of the house a door stood half open. Empty bottles, rusty tins, and the remains of a meal lay in the yard near the door.

Roberto nudged Felipe and pointed at the door. "Let's go inside and have a look," he urged. He walked to the door and stuck his head around the corner. Inside, in the half darkness, it smelled musty. He couldn't see anyone.

"Is someone there?" Roberto cried out.

"Is it you, Pepe?" a voice called back from the darkness.

The question was so unexpected that Roberto did not know what to say. Then he answered, "No, it's Roberto."

"Has the truck come?" the same voice asked again.

"The truck?" repeated Roberto, baffled. "No, I don't know about a truck."

"Leave me in peace then, damnation. I told you to call me when the truck arrived, understand? Now scram."

Roberto remained standing there, stupidly. Felipe repressed a giggle.

Roberto turned to him. "Don't laugh so idiotically," he snapped at Felipe.

"But it was so funny when you suddenly got an answer. I was dumbfounded too, you know," Felipe explained.

Roberto did not answer. He stared at the house, but the owner of the voice did not show himself. It remained silent inside.

Felipe looked around. "Where is that boat then?" he asked. "Shall we explore a bit?" They wandered about the yard and looked everywhere.

Perhaps they were just fooling me, as they did with that tomato crate, thought Roberto, but he did not say so aloud.

"I don't see anything," said Felipe.

"No, I don't either," answered Roberto.

"Perhaps farther in the plantation," suggested Felipe. "Are you coming?"

They picked their way through the greenery. The ground was very uneven. They climbed hills and searched in valleys where the heat hung between the high plants. Insects hummed in their ears, and a lizard rustled away between dry leaves.

"It's strange all the same that we don't see anyone," said Felipe. "Do you think it was Manuel el Bobo in that house? It's a mess there, I must say."

Roberto crawled through the low-hanging leaves, peering in all directions. They arrived at a narrow, trampled path along which the bunches of bananas could be transported to the yard. Almost at once the boys saw the boat lying in a small ditch by the side of the path.

"There it is," said Felipe triumphantly.

"I was afraid . . . ." Roberto did not finish his sentence. He walked toward the boat, and his hand felt the hull.

The boat was very neglected. The bottom was rotten, the stern was splayed and there wasn't a speck of paint on it.

"Too bad," said Felipe. "She looks as if she had been a pretty boat once."

"The frame is still good," Roberto said slowly. "Perhaps she can be repaired."

"Perhaps," agreed Felipe.

They examined the boat closely. Behind them the broad leaves of the banana plants parted, and a grubby face peered through the green. A pair of hostile eyes watched them. For a moment the ragged lout remained motionless in the bushes. Then he approached silently, moving like a cat, his bare feet making no sound. He stood just behind the boys.

Felipe bent over and tapped at the boat. "Yes, you could at least try to fix it up."

"What do you want to try, and what are you doing here?"

The boys jerked around, their knees knocking. They looked into a sinister face with cold eyes.

"Speak up. What are you doing here?" the lout snapped at them. He took a step forward. His shoulder touched Roberto's.

"We wanted . . . we came . . . we heard there was a boat here," stammered Roberto. "I thought. . . ."

"I don't care what you thought. You have no business here. Scram!" the boy snarled. He pushed the two boys along the narrow path to the yard. He was carrying a large machete. Robert felt its leather sheath touch his thigh.

In the yard Roberto turned to him. "You aren't the overseer of the plantation, are you?" he said.

"Is that any of your business?" barked the lout. "You'd better keep your big mouth shut and get out of here!"

From the direction of the house there was a noise as a lean man stood in the doorway. He peered groggily at the group in the yard and staggered toward them. "What's the matter?" he asked. "What's it all about, Pepe?"

"I found these grasshoppers on the plantation, Father," said Pepe.

"Are you perhaps Manuel el . . . ." Roberto hastily swallowed the last word. "Are you Manuel, the overseer of this plantation?"

The man peered at Roberto with his small, watery eyes. "I'm the manager, yes," he said.

"I came to look at that old boat. I wanted. . . ."

Manuel el Bobo didn't listen. He looked at Pepe. "Did you tell him about that boat?" he asked.

"I? No, I didn't say anything," said Pepe.

Manuel el Bobo looked suspiciously at his son.

"We came to find out if it was for sale," said Roberto quickly.

"You came all that way for an old wreck?" asked Manuel el Bobo. He began to snigger.

I don't think he's all there, thought Felipe, looking around nervously.

"I told them to get the hell out of here," said Pepe.

Manuel el Bobo turned on him. "Are you still here?" he snarled. "And what about the bananas? Are they in the yard yet? If I were you, I'd get a move on."

Pepe crept away.

"Let's go, Roberto," muttered Felipe. He did not want to be left alone with Manuel el Bobo.

But now Roberto had got to the plantation he wanted to complete his business. "Won't you sell me your boat?" he asked Manuel el Bobo.

Manuel shook his head. "That would be difficult," he said. "The boat isn't mine. I'm the manager of this plantation. I have to take care the bananas get to town. What a lot of work! And the boys don't help me. They are lazy pigs." He spat on the ground.

"But the boat. . . ." Roberto insisted stubbornly.

"The boat belongs to the *señor*. I have nothing to say about it." Manuel el Bobo wiped his mouth with the back of his hand. "They may say what they like about

Manuel," he observed gloomily. "Everyone has his faults. But I'm honest. I take care of the *señor's* business. I do my best. No one can criticize me."

The boys looked at the untidy yard, the shabby house, and the neglected plantation. They had their own thoughts about him.

"We'd better be going," said Roberto.

"Yes," said Manuel. "It's no good here in the yard with this heat. It makes a man thirsty." He shuffled back into the house.

Roberto and Felipe walked around the house till they came to the path that led to the highway. As they went down it a big truck came swaying and bumping from the opposite direction.

"There's the truck! They'd better hurry with their bananas," jeered Felipe.

"Yes." Roberto grinned. "Pepe is a fine one to act so big. A pity Manuel el Bobo can't sell us that old boat."

"I think he is crazy," said Felipe seriously.

"He's a poor wretch," said Roberto. "He thinks that he's a hard worker and a good manager as well. But he's sold his soul to the bottle. That's plain enough."

The boys had reached the highway. It wasn't long before a truck overtook them and gave them a lift into town. The hanging clock in the living room chimed nine times as the boys entered the house.

Don Pablo and Doña María were not at home. But Emperatriz stood in the kitchen as if she had never left it.

6

THE FLIGHT

Roberto and Felipe sat on the floor of Roberto's garage. They were fiddling with the outboard motor and had it partly assembled, but couldn't make it catch.

"It's hopeless," said Roberto. He threw the wrench on the ground.

"It's getting dark," said Felipe. "Let's stop."

Roberto began to gather his tools together. "As soon as Ordulio puts in, I'll take the whole thing to the factory," he said.

"Where do these tools go?" asked Felipe.

"In the toolbox in the closet of the ironing shed," answered Roberto.

They left the garage. Twilight had fallen. The birds sat huddled in their cage. At the back of the yard Emperatriz's hut and the ironing shed were nestled in shrubbery. It was dark already there. When the boys entered the ironing shed, they saw a yellow strip of light shining around the door of one of the closets.

"There's a light in that closet," said Felipe.

"That's silly. There can't be." Roberto put down the tools and tugged at the door. It was stuck.

"Is it locked?" asked Felipe. "What kind of light can it be?"

"Help me pull," ordered Roberto. "It's not locked; it's stuck. This closet is never used."

They pulled at the door. It opened suddenly. On the floor of the closet stood a burning candle, which flickered in the sudden draft.

"Did you ever? A candle!" said Roberto, surprised.

"Look there, behind the candle," whispered Felipe. The boys crouched on the ground in front of the closet. On the back wall they saw a dirty snapshot, tacked upside down. They looked at it with widened eyes.

At last Roberto said, "It's Aníbal."

"What?"

"It's a photograph of Aníbal," repeated Roberto.

"A photograph of Aníbal? How did it get here? Why is it upside down? And what's the candle for?" asked Felipe in one breath.

In the dark little ironing shed the boys looked at each other. The candle threw a fitful light on their faces.

"I don't know," said Roberto finally. "But I imagine Emperatriz knows something about this. I think it has a connection with her trip to the Isle of the Skull!"

"Do you think that medicine man . . . ."

"Salomon," said Roberto.

"Yes, Salomon. Do you think that he told her that she had to put a photograph of Aníbal upside down in a closet with a burning candle in front of it?"

Roberto nodded.

"But why? For what reason?"

"I don't know," said Roberto.

"I think it's stupid. It could start a fire," said Felipe practically.

"Yes, you're right," agreed Roberto. He stretched out his hand to extinguish the candle.

Behind him a voice said coldly, "Leave it!" Startled, the boys turned around. In the dark doorway of the ironing shed stood Emperatriz.

"Emperatriz," said Roberto, "you scared me half to death. Did you put that photograph there, and the candle?"

"Yes," said Emperatriz.

"But why . . . ?"

"Just because," said Emperatriz. When the boys gaped at her, she burst out, "Aníbal is gone. No one knows where! He is a good-for-nothing, but he's my brother. That's the reason. Do you understand? I want him back!"

"Have you been to Salomon? Has he told you that if you put a picture of Aníbal upside down with a burning candle in front of it, he'll come back?" asked Roberto.

"Yes," Emperatriz said simply, not at all surprised that the boys knew of her visit to the witch doctor.

"I hope he's right," Felipe remarked. Emperatriz fixed her gaze on him, saying nothing. In the ironing shed the silence was oppressive. Felipe wriggled uncomfortably. Roberto said quickly. "Yes, I hope Aníbal will return soon. He half promised to take me in his boat along the coast. I want to go to the sawmill in the jungle."

"The jungle. . . ." whispered Emperatriz. She stared at Roberto with big, alarmed eyes. "You don't want to go to the jungle!"

Baffled by this sudden reaction, the boys were silent. Emperatriz bent over. The flickering candle lit her broad face. Her eyes opened wide. Hoarsely she whispered, "Don't ever go into the jungle, do you hear? There are wild woods, *selvas bravas,* all along the coast. It's dangerous."

Roberto nodded. "I know there are many snakes," he said.

"I did not mean that," Emperatriz said hoarsely. Her voice sounded ominous. "Those woods themselves are dangerous. Cruel woods, which take you and won't give you back. It's a maze of waterways, rivers, swamps, and creeks. A drowned land, which you float into, and then the water suddenly withdraws and you're stuck in the mire. Your canoe is lying motionless in the muddy bottom of a creek or the stinking green of a morass, and no one can hear you when you call, for the woods are lonely. Lonely and vast. No one hears you when you call!"

Roberto shrugged his shoulders. "Of course, the water recedes," he said. "That's when the tide turns, and it goes back to sea. There's about a thirteen-foot difference between ebb and flood tide. At ebb tide a large part of the coast runs dry. So if you enter a creek that runs dry at ebb tide, you're stranded, of course."

Emperatriz shook her head. "They are *selvas bravas,* dangerous, wild woods. Many a person has lost his life there, I'm telling you."

"But if we go with Aníbal, there will be three of us," Felipe said coaxingly.

Emperatriz's lips curled contemptuously. "You think you're safe with three, eh? Don't you know that once five people vanished in the woods at the same time? Five! The woods never gave them back."

"Did the people all die?" asked Roberto.

"Ah," said Emperatriz. "It happened about five years ago. They were people from Bogotá—five men, if I remember rightly. They wanted to hunt wild ducks in the jungle. Everyone warned them, but they went anyway." Emperatriz shook her head and fell silent.

"And then?" asked Felipe.

"Then? Nothing. They never returned."

"But doesn't anyone know what happened to them? Didn't they search for them?" asked Roberto.

"Yes, they did," Emperatriz said slowly. "People went to look for them. But they never found a trace of them. The mists hanging over the swamps, between the trees, seemed to have dissolved them. But a year later. . . ." Emperatriz stroked her face with her flat hand.

"Yes," whispered Roberto and Felipe.

"A year later a woodsman told a strange story. He had gone farther than usual into the rain forest, and he had seen a human being there, completely mad and stark naked. People say he was the only survivor of the group of hunters and that he lost his reason. The poor fellow. Perhaps he's still roaming around in the jungle. Who can tell?" Emperatriz fell silent.

The two boys gazed ahead quietly. It must be terrible, thought Roberto, to wander alone through the jungle like a lost spirit.

From the dark yard came the voice of Doña María. "Emperatriz, Roberto, Felipe. Where are you!"

"Aha," said Emperatriz. "You have to go inside. Dinner has been ready for a long time." She turned and walked back to the kitchen. The boys followed.

The next day, when Don Pablo came home for lunch, he brought the news that the *Villeta,* the *Buga,* and the *Pereira* had put in that morning. Directly after the meal the boys hoisted the outboard motor into the back of the car. They need not have hurried for Don Pablo first had several errands in town. Later in the afternoon they drove to the factory.

It had been raining. A mist hung over the water, and the rain forest at the other side of the river was almost blotted out. It was a gloomy, moist day, oppressively hot. The boats at the pier lay low in the water. Under the pier the gray mud strip was visible. Among the slimy piles under the factory darkness reigned. A canoe appeared out of the mist and disappeared a moment later into the many mangrove islands. The air roots of the mangroves stuck out of the mud like bony fingers.

As always, there was a crowd around the landing stage.

"Which one is Ordulio?" asked Felipe, looking around.

"I haven't seen him yet. But there are the *Villeta,* the *Buga,* and the *Pereira.* Oh, there comes Ordulio."

Ordulio emerged from the engine room and stepped on deck.

"Hey, Ordulio. How are you!" shouted Roberto.

"Ola, Roberto! How are you! What's the news?" Ordulio called back.

"I've brought my outboard motor!"

Ordulio laughed. "All right. Bring it here." He climbed on the landing stage. Roberto and Felipe hurried to get the outboard motor from the back of the car and bring it to the pier. They put it in a corner behind the scales, where it wasn't in anybody's way. Ordulio brought some tools from the boat. He inspected the motor thoughtfully and tried to start it. Then he began to dismantle it expertly.

The boys sat watching him. Roberto sighed with satisfaction. At last the motor was in good hands.

"Have you been the engineer on the *Villeta* for long?" asked Felipe.

"A little while," answered Ordulio without looking up.

"You're not from the coast. Where do you come from?" Felipe continued.

Ordulio rummaged with his fingers among the screws and bolts, making no answer. Finally he said, "I'm missing a screw, Roberto."

Roberto got up. "Shall I look in the car? Maybe it was left there," he said. "Are you coming, Felipe?"

They went to the car and found the screw. But when they returned to the pier, Ordulio wasn't there. "Where has he gone?" asked Roberto.

"Perhaps he went to get something from the boat," suggested Felipe.

A black girl who stood washing shrimps close by said, "They've come to get him. He had to go to your father's office."

"My father's office?" Roberto echoed stupidly. "What does he have to do there?"

The girl shrugged her shoulders. "Who knows?" she said indifferently.

"Let's go and look," proposed Felipe.

They entered the factory. Women were busy sorting and packing shrimps. They chattered loudly. Two women, who were quarreling, hurled insults at each other. The other women laughed shrilly.

The office was behind the factory. It was a big room, divided into two by a wooden partition. In the first cubicle sat the two typists. Behind the partition was Don Pablo's office.

As soon as the boys entered, they noticed that something was wrong. The typists were whispering mysteriously. Now and then they looked furtively at the door in the partition.

"Is Ordulio here?" asked Roberto.

One of the typists put her finger to her lips. She nodded vigorously.

"But why . . . ?"

"Hush, keep quiet." She glanced at the partition, which did not reach all the way to the ceiling. "The police are here," she whispered. "They asked for him."

At that moment the voice of one of the policemen rose clearly, "Well, answer me. You are Ordulio Gabriel Torres, aren't you?"

There was an indistinguishable murmur.

"You come from the state of Boyaca and were last domiciled in Tunja?"

Again Ordulio's voice could be heard, but the boys could not make out what he said.

"We have been ordered to arrest you for the murder of. . . ." The policeman got not farther. There was a shrill cry in the office and a noise of furniture being thrown over. Roberto and Felipe ran to the door and pulled it open. They reached it just in time to see Ordulio leap through the window and disappear.

When the policemen got to the window, Ordulio was already out of sight. He had dived under the factory and was lost in the dark forest of green, slimy piles.

7

PURSUIT ON THE DAGUA RIVER

In the middle of the night Roberto woke up. He sat up straight in bed. Outside the palms rustled; otherwise it was still.

What's the matter? thought Roberto. Then he knew. His outboard motor! In the excitement of Ordulio's escape he had forgotten it and left it on the pier. I hope it's still there, thought Roberto. There's so much theft these days.

The more he thought about it, the more worried he became. At last he could not stay in bed any longer. He got up quietly and began to search for his clothes in the darkness.

Felipe woke up. "What's the matter? What are you doing?" he asked.

"Hush," whispered Roberto. "Don't talk so loudly."

"But what are you doing?" persisted Felipe in a lower tone.

"I'm going to the factory."

"To the factory? Now? Are you crazy?" asked Felipe.

"Hush, you'll wake everyone," scolded Roberto. "Yes, I'm going to the factory. I forgot to bring my outboard motor home yesterday, and I'm afraid it will be stolen. I'm going to get it."

"But isn't there a night watchman?"

"Yes, but he sleeps all the time. And if he heard something, he wouldn't look to see what it was. No, I'm going there myself. I can't sleep anymore."

Felipe sighed and got out of bed.

"What are you doing?" asked Roberto.

"I'm going with you, of course. Did you think I'd let you go alone?" He began to dress himself too.

A moment later they slipped out of the window into the dark garden. They climbed over the garden gate and walked through the still, sleeping town toward the factory. The sky was overcast; a single star twinkled through a narrow gap between the clouds.

"Stupid of me to forget the motor," Roberto grumbled, as they walked over the deserted road.

"I didn't think of it either," said Felipe. "I was frightened when I saw Ordulio jump through the window like a jaguar!"

"Yes, it's awful. Who would have thought that Ordulio . . . ?" Roberto's voice faded away.

"You've always said you liked him so much."

"I did. Ordulio was kind to me. I liked him a lot. Perhaps the policemen are mistaken. Perhaps it isn't true. . . ."

"But they knew his exact name and where he lived and everything."

"That's true."

"And when I asked him where he came from, he didn't answer. Do you remember? He wouldn't tell anything about himself. And if it isn't true, why did he run away?"

"Yes," agreed Roberto. "I can't bear to think that all that time old Josué was sailing . . . well . . . with a murderer on board."

"Perhaps he's creeping around the neighborhood," said Felipe. "That's even worse. As long as no one knew about him, he would want to stay out of trouble. But now he is unmasked and people are after him, so he may be dangerous. A hunted person is capable of anything."

"Yes," said Roberto. "Just like a wild animal. When it's cornered, it attacks."

"Exactly," agreed Felipe.

They walked on over the lonely dark road. Their footsteps sounded hollowly. The water rippled under the pile dwellings. Sometimes they caught a glimpse of the river between the dark hovels.

"Do you think they'll get him?"

"I don't know. You can go a long way underneath those pilings without being seen, and there are always places to hide."

"He may even be in the neighborhood here."

"Yes."

"Hush. Quiet."

"What's the matter?"

"I thought I heard something." They stood still and listened.

"I don't hear anything," said Roberto. "Let's go on."

"They never found a trace of Aníbal either," said Felipe, as they continued on their way. "What do you think he has done?"

"I don't know. I've a feeling that it has something to do with Ling Pa. Perhaps Aníbal stole something, and Ling Pa told on him."

"That's quite possible. I don't trust Ling Pa."

In the gray darkness the factory loomed up in front of them. "Thank goodness, we're here," sighed Felipe. All was quiet. Only the motors of the refrigerators hummed softly. The gate was closed, but the boys easily scaled it.

"Didn't I tell you? That night watchman hears nothing," grumbled Roberto.

"Sh . . . don't wake him," whispered Felipe. They giggled softly. Then they crept through the long, dark factory passage. The night watchman was nowhere to be seen. No wonder. He lay sleeping peacefully as usual on a heap of nets in the attic.

At the end of the passage the river showed as a gray blur. Felipe stumbled against a chest on which a wire shrimp basket stood. The basket overturned and clattered to the floor. From the dark water a canoe shot between the pilings and hit the pier.

Roberto and Felipe went to the landing stage. The *Villeta,* the *Buga,* and the *Pereira* lay like small whales in the water. Everywhere it was dark and silent.

"Here," whispered Roberto. "Here . . . behind the scales." Then he uttered a shriek. "Felipe! It's gone!"

"What? It can't be true!"

"See for yourself. It's not there anymore. It's stolen." Tears came to his eyes. Though he had weighed the possibility, he hadn't really believed he would not find the motor.

Felipe looked around. "Perhaps it fell in the water," he said hesitantly.

"Do you think so?" Roberto asked hopefully. That would be better than having it stolen. His glance slid over the dark water. It was high tide. There was only a meter or so between the surface of the water and the top of the wooden pier. Roberto began to take off his clothes.

"What are you going to do?" asked Felipe.

"Dive, of course." Roberto let himself slide into the

water and dove under the surface. Felipe remained alone on the dark landing stage. The water rippled softly against the piles. Under the pier he suddenly heard a noise. What was it? He listened carefully. There it was again! A slight sound as if something had rubbed against the piles under the pier. Something was moving in there! Without making a noise, Felipe lay down on his stomach on the pier. He bent his head far over the edge and tried to pierce the darkness with his eyes. But between the piles under the pier it was so dark that he could see nothing. Yet. . . .

Roberto surfaced spluttering. "Couldn't find anything," he said.

"Roberto," whispered Felipe. "Someone is under the pier."

"What?"

"I heard a noise under the pier. Someone is there."

Roberto peered under the landing stage. "Where?" he asked.

Just then there was the sound of a paddle in the water. At the other end of the pier a canoe slipped between the moored fishing boats upriver.

Felipe ran out. "Roberto, there he goes!"

"With my motor!" panted Roberto. "Watch him, Felipe. I'll come in a second!" Quickly he swam the short distance to one of the huts next to the factory. A moment later he returned in a canoe.

"Hurry, get in. We're going after him," he said grimly. Felipe lowered himself into the canoe. They paddled up the dark river.

"Which direction did he take?"

"I don't know exactly. Upstream, I think," said Felipe. They peered over the water. Wide and lonely, the river flowed under the gray clouds. The water glinted dully. The jungle along the far shore formed an inky fringe.

"I believe I see something there," said Felipe. "Can't you go a little faster? We'll never overtake him this way."

"I can't go faster. Can you help me? Is there a punting pole in the boat?" panted Roberto. But there wasn't. Roberto paddled with all his might.

"I don't see anything anymore. I think he's paddling near the shore, in the shadow of the jungle." Some trees, standing far into the water, loomed in front of them.

"Do you see anything?"

"No."

Roberto let his paddle rest for a moment.

"Shall I take over?" offered Felipe.

"Please." They changed places. Felipe paddled, and Roberto scanned the water. Suddenly a brilliant beam of light hit the canoe. The boys were blinded by it.

A small boat came alongside. "Customs!" called a voice. "Who are you? What are you doing here?"

"We . . . we. . . ." squeaked Roberto and Felipe, with scared voices. The light slid searchingly over the canoe.

"It's empty. They're just boys. You're Roberto, aren't you?" one of the officers asked.

"Yes, and this is Felipe, Don Luís's son," Roberto added hastily.

The customs officer grinned. "That's a fine kettle of fish. What are you doing here without any clothes on?"

The boys recounted what had happened. "Didn't you see the canoe?" asked Roberto at last.

The officers shook their heads. "By now the canoe could be in town. You may be sure that the outboard motor has already landed in Venice."

"Can't you turn off that light?" asked Roberto. In its fierce glare he began to feel more and more naked. He was also getting cold. It was beginning to rain.

The customs men did not hold them up any longer. They put out their searchlight and moved off.

"I was scared stiff when the light came on like that," said Felipe. "I forgot that the river is guarded. That's because of the smugglers, of course."

"Probably," said Roberto listlessly. He thought of his outboard motor. He did not dare tell his father what had happened.

Silently they paddled back in the rain.

Yes, the rivers were guarded, but the nights were long. On the water it was chilly and dark for the customs men. Often they could not resist the temptation of taking a bottle of *aguardiente* along, to shorten the time and to chase the cold.

And the smugglers profited. Quietly they sailed with their dangerous cargo over the dark water and were lost in the depths of night.

More and more weapons entered the country.

8

AT LA BOCANA

The palms of La Bocana rustled in the sea breeze. The waves of the Pacific Ocean washed gently over the narrow strand. The sand was black, and there was much bleached driftwood strewn about. In the shadow of the palms and of the jungle behind them stood a row of huts. They faced the beach and most of them displayed a board on which *Restaurant* was written. Day visitors could eat there on Sundays, and they could buy lemonade, beer, and candy.

The bungalow of Felipe's parents stood a bit farther back. Its construction was the same as that of the other huts, but it was larger and freshly painted. Roberto and Felipe walked together along the narrow, black beach, their feet in the lukewarm water. They had been at La Bocana for ten days and had been having a wonderful time.

"What luck, that your mother agreed to come here after all," said Roberto for the hundreth time.

"It was too much for Father to drive back and forth to Cali," answered Felipe.

They walked to the bungalow. Doña Cecilia sat in front of the bungalow under an almond tree, which was shaped like an umbrella.

"There you are," she said. "Where are the others? I haven't seen anyone the whole afternoon."

"We swam and walked along the beach," answered Felipe. "Mercedes is with her friend. They're looking for those hulls from the jicra palms. I don't know where David and José are."

At that moment Mercedes came with her friend Gloria around the corner of the bungalow. They had a basket with them full of long brown sheaths, like stockings with pointed feet. They were the outer wrappings of the fruit of the jicra palm, woven by nature into a fine, elastic web, and they fell on the ground after the fruit had ripened.

"Are you going to make caps with them?" Doña Cecilia asked, smiling.

"Yes. But Mother, David and José have climbed a palm tree in back of the house. They have a big hatchet, and they're cutting off the leaves with it. I told them to come down, but they won't listen."

Doña Cecilia hurried to the back.

"Tattletale. Let the boys climb, if they want to," said Felipe to his sister.

"You mind your own business. If they fall, Mother has the problem," snapped Mercedes. Behind the house they heard the voice of Doña Cecilia.

"David, José. Come down at once with that big hatchet. It's too dangerous. Do you hear?"

Roberto and Felipe went behind the house too. Between the bungalow and the jungle stood banana and papaya trees and a few high coconut palms. David sat in a slender palm, waving a hatchet bigger than himself. José had already climbed down.

"David, listen. Come down immediately!" cried Doña Cecilia again.

"But we want to make a hut, and we need palm leaves for the roof," David shouted back.

"I don't care what you need them for. Come down!" commanded Doña Cecilia. Grumbling, David slid down like a lizard.

"You could have hurt yourself badly if you had fallen. And where did you get that hatchet?"

"From Pedro's shed," said David. He ran off with José.

Pedro and his wife Marta were two very old Negroes. Pedro did not have a tooth in his mouth anymore, and Marta was so thin that her skin wrinkled around her. They lived the whole year round in a little room behind the kitchen. Marta took care of the house, Pedro repaired something now and then, and, when the family was there, Marta cooked.

"May we have a Coca-Cola, Mother?" asked Felipe.

"Yes, if you get it yourself. We've no more in the house," answered Doña Cecilia. Armed with a big basket, the boys went into one of the huts to buy Coca-Cola and lemonade. When they came back, Doña Cecilia, Mercedes, and Gloria had disappeared.

"They've gone for a walk," said Marta. "And David and José are back in the tree!"

Seated on a piece of driftwood, the boys drank their Cokes. They gazed across the sea. A ship lay waiting at the entrance to Buenaventura Bay. The pilot would have to guide it between sandbanks and cliffs to bring it safely into the harbor.

A canoe with two fishermen slid into the open sea. Swiftly and supplely the two men drove the long narrow boat through the waves. The boys followed them a long time with their eyes.

"I'd like to do that," said Roberto.

"Father's canoe is under the porch, at the back of the house. Want to come and look?"

"O.K."

Except for the bedrooms, the bungalow was completely open. They crossed the porch, went down the steps at the back, and looked under the house. Between the piles lay a canoe.

"The paddle and the punting pole are inside," said Felipe.

"Shall we use it? We could paddle to the mouth of the Raposo River. There are a lot of little islands there," said Roberto.

They pulled the canoe over the strand and pushed it into the water. Felipe stepped into the stern with the paddle. Roberto poled the canoe through the waves in the bow. He didn't do as well as the fishermen, but well enough to keep from being swamped.

They paddled alongside the ship and shouted a greeting to the crew.

Roberto warned Felipe, "Don't go too far from the shore."

Presently they rounded the Printa Soldado, a spit of land opposite La Bocana. They paddled on, close under the forested coast. One moment their canoe was lifted up by an oncoming wave; then it was plunged into a green, watery valley.

Felipe let his paddle rest a moment. He bent over the edge of the canoe and let his arm dangle in the water.

Roberto looked back. "Take care!" he said. "Next moment you'll lose it."

"What? My paddle? I'm taking care of it."

"No, your arm. There might be sharks here."

"Not so close to the coast," said Felipe, but he pulled his arm in anyway.

"I'm not so sure. You should listen to the stories of the men at our factory. They say the hammerhead sharks sometimes dive under your canoe and capsize it."

"Do you believe them?"

"I don't know. But the sandbanks and reefs are dangerous too. When a boat gets stuck on the rocks that they call the Ships' Grave, it never gets off. It's beaten to pieces. A lot of ships have been wrecked there."

"How terrible," said Felipe. He looked over the water. The waves came rolling in with a soft hissing sound. The sea looked calm and safe. The coastline curved far outwards, edged by the jungle and disappearing into the horizon.

"Do you think we'll get to the Raposo soon?" asked Felipe after a while.

"I don't know. I believe it's behind that point of land, but I've never been there either." They paddled on. When they approached the point, another canoe came into sight and passed them, keeping close to shore.

Felipe waved his paddle, and Roberto shouted a greeting, but the man in the canoe didn't show any sign of having seen them.

They paddled rapidly on, forgetting the stranger until

they heard a shrill cry behind them. Startled, they looked back. The canoe that had just passed them had capsized, and the man was trying desperately to pull himself up on it. Again and again he slipped back into the water.

"Help! Help!" he screamed.

"Roberto, he's drowning. We have to help him. Quick!" With some trouble the boys turned their canoe and paddled to the spot where the canoe had gone over. A big wave was rolling over the man and the canoe. A second wave threw them on the beach where the man lay motionless, his face in the sand. Landing their canoe near the capsized one, the boys ran to the man and bent over him.

"He's not drowned. He's breathing," said Roberto.

"Are you hurt?" Felipe asked the man anxiously.

"Can we do something for you?" asked Roberto.

The man gave no sign of life.

"Something must have knocked him unconscious," said Felipe. "Should we turn him over, so he can breathe better?"

"They always say not to move someone who's been hurt in an accident in case something is broken," said Roberto.

"What do we do then?" asked Felipe.

"Get help, and quickly," said Roberto. He scanned the deserted beach, the empty sea. Then he looked again at the prostrate figure at his feet. The man was evidently not a fisherman. He wore gray flannel trousers and a colorful shirt. In a way he looked familiar. Roberto let out a surprised whistle. "Felipe," he said. "Do you know who this is!"

"How should I?" Felipe answered nervously.

"Well, I do. He's the man who gave me the fifty dollars," said Roberto.

"The one who lost his wallet?"

"The same one. I recognize his shirt! We must find help."

"But where?" asked Felipe.

"We can paddle to that ship we saw in the mouth of the bay and ask if they have a doctor on board."

"Let's hurry then," said Felipe.

They went back to their canoe, pushed it into the water, jumped in, and paddled back as fast as they could.

But from afar they noticed that the ship was no longer lying where they had left it. They arrived just in time to see it sail majestically into the bay. Its screw made a broad, foaming trail in the water.

"Oh, Felipe, what shall we do now?" Roberto asked. "It will take too long to paddle all the way to Buenaventura. We can't leave that poor fellow alone on the beach all that time." Since the man had given him the fifty dollars, Roberto felt especially responsible for him.

"Let's go to the bungalow and ask Mother's advice," said Felipe.

Roberto nodded. There was nothing better to do.

They paddled back to the beach in front of the bungalow.

Doña Cecilia sat with the two girls on the porch. They

were making caps out of the brown hulls of the jicra palm. Carefully they stretched out the fine webbing and rolled over the edge. Finished, a hull resembled a funny elf's cap.

Felipe and Roberto stormed onto the porch and told them what had happened.

Doña Cecilia jumped up. "Something will have to be done at once," she said. She reflected a moment. "Let's go to the landing stage and see if we can find someone to get help in town."

They all ran to the ramshackle wooden dock on the bay.

Before Felipe had reached it, he saw a small motorboat approach across the water. "Father," he cried joyously. "It's Father!"

The boys ran up to the dock and before Don Luís could get out they told him their story.

Don Luís listened attentively. Then he said, "There's no sense getting a doctor. That takes far too long, and we don't know what's the matter with the man. We'll go there at once in my boat. I know something about first aid, and if necessary we can take him into town. That seems simpler and quicker." He turned to Alvaro, the skipper, who was listening with open mouth.

A moment later they plowed out of the bay and into the sea. It was a still clear evening. The sun gave off fan-shaped rays of color as it sank. The jungle stood silhouetted against the bright sky. The sea caught the last sunbeams as the oncoming waves melted into a path of gold. Like a fiery ball the sun disappeared into the sea, a sight seldom seen, for usually a cloud bank hid the sun before it reached the horizon. It grew dark quickly. The motorboat throbbed through the water. A broad foamy wake fanned out behind them.

"It was here somewhere," said Felipe.

"No, a little farther, I think," argued Roberto.

Don Luís gave a sign to the skipper. The motorboat swerved in to the coast. Alvaro remained in the boat. Don Luís, Felipe, and Roberto jumped out and waded ashore. They looked around searchingly.

"This way. A little to the right," said Roberto.

He walked on and then stood still. "He's gone!" he cried.

"We went too far just as I said," grumbled Felipe. He walked back along the dark beach.

"There! There!" He pointed at a dark object on the sand. They ran to it.

"It's only a tree trunk," said Roberto.

"Perhaps still a bit farther?" Felipe hesitated.

"I thought he was right here."

"With the motorboat the distance seems much shorter, of course," said Don Luís. "We'll search some more."

They looked thoroughly over a wide area. Often they thought they saw the motionless figure of a man on the beach, and then it turned out to be another piece of driftwood.

The boys were completely confused, and Don Luís began to lose his patience. He was tired and hungry.

"I don't know how you feel, boys, but I want to go home. There isn't any man."

"But we saw him. He's got to be here!" cried the boys.

Don Luís shrugged his shoulders. He waded back to the boat, and the boys didn't know what else to do but follow him.

They went back to the landing stage and walked along the dark beach to the bungalow. A little oil lamp burned on the porch. Mosquitoes hummed around it. David and José were gathering driftwood on the beach.

"We're going to make a campfire and fry fish!" they shouted.

Soon the fire flared up, and a big pan of fish and bananas were frying above it.

Don Luís and Doña Cecilia sat on folding chairs. The children grouped themselves in a circle on the moist sand. The palms rustled. The sea wind brushed the rain forest, the dark vast jungle where thousands of waterways met in a weird pattern. The sea murmured. The small sickle of the moon, which had showed earlier in the evening, vanished. In the night-blue sky stars twinkled. And under these bright little stars, the boats of the smugglers found their way.

9

IN LING PA'S WAREHOUSE

Felipe poked the dying fire. "I think it's queer," he said. "What can have happened to the fellow?"

"I don't understand it at all," said Roberto.

"It's certainly strange," grumbled Don Luís. "Was there really a man?"

"Of course, Roberto recognized him," Felipe cried indignantly.

"Recognized him? Who was it?" asked Don Luís.

"I don't know. I recognized his shirt," answered Roberto.

"His shirt? And what about his face?"

"I didn't see it. He lay face down. Isn't that right, Felipe?"

"Yes," nodded Felipe.

"As if there weren't other shirts made of the same material," scoffed Don Luís. "I think your imagination has been working overtime."

The boys, insulted, kept quiet.

Marta appeared on the porch with two demitasses. Don Luís and Doña Cecilia went back to drink their coffee. Mercedes and Gloria ran after them, and David and José were called to bed.

Pedro came around the corner of the bungalow with a coconut in his hands. He went to the two boys, who sat sullenly on the beach together.

"Want a drink?" he asked. He took the plug out of a hole in the nut and passed it to Felipe.

Felipe drank. "This isn't just cocomilk," he said. "What is it?"

Pedro grinned toothlessly. "Nice, isn't it?" he said, pleased. "We added wild honey and cinnamon and *aguardiente*, and we buried it for twenty days." He let Roberto taste it too, and then began to drink greedily.

Roberto's thoughts were still with the adventure of the afternoon. "Perhaps he was washed away by a wave," he said. "We should have dragged him farther up the beach."

"You said not to touch him," Felipe pointed out. "Anyway it's stupid to go out in a canoe if you can't swim. How do you think the accident happened. Do you think a hammerhead overturned the canoe?"

Roberto shrugged his shoulders. "We'll never know now," he said.

"Sometimes strange things happen," declared Pedro. He gave the coconut once more to the boys and said, "I hear César Gomez lost two of his boats at sea. Has any more been heard about them?"

"Not a word," said Roberto.

"Ah," said Pedro slowly. "He may be a great gentleman now, but he comes out of a stinking nest. His father was a bad one."

"Oh?" asked Roberto, immediately interested.

"Yes, I knew him well," said Pedro. "Bigote, we called him. He was as big as a tree with a great big black mustache. He knew no pity and didn't spare anyone. The man had no conscience. He came to a bad end, though."

"What happened to him?" asked Roberto.

"Ah!" said Pedro. "Bigote became very rich by smuggling. He smuggled anything he could find into the country. He knew the coast like no one else. One night he was discovered accidentally by two fishermen far at sea. Bigote sailed so close with his boat that he capsized them."

"How awful! Why did he do that?"

"So they couldn't betray him. But one man managed to swim ashore. It was a miracle, for as I said they were a long way from land and there were many sharks."

"I suppose that man reported him," said Felipe.

Pedro nodded. "Yes, Bigote died in prison."

Roberto gave a deep sigh. At last he had heard the story of Gomez's father here at La Bocana!

Dark clouds were massing overhead. No star was to be seen anymore. The first raindrops began to fall. The boys and Pedro ran to the bungalow. A moment later it was pouring. Standing on the porch, they stared at the curtain of water.

"It may get quite bad tonight," said Don Luís.

"Yes, *señor,*" agreed Pedro. "There are nights when the rainfall is twenty centimeters!"

Marta brought a few candles. The boys went to bed.

In the bungalow the roof began to leak in several places. Thick drops splashed on the wooden floor. The rain drummed on the roof, flushed through the wide gutters, and splashed into the rain barrels around the house. The trees in the forest dripped. The sound of rain filled the night.

Listening to its patter and to the hissing of the surf, the boys fell asleep.

The next day Doña Cecilia said, "Felipe, you'll have to go into town with your father. I need supplies: potatoes, rice, matches, meat, and butter. I've made a list."

Felipe made a face. He did not want to go.

Noticing, Doña Cecilia said, "If you divide the shopping it won't take much time. Perhaps Alvaro can bring you back early."

Half an hour later Roberto and Felipe went with Don Luís and Alvaro to town in the motorboat. A morning mist hung over the water. The woods along the shore were hazy blue. They could hardly see the little town at the end of the bay.

When they stepped ashore, their paths separated. Felipe first went with his father to the post office to see if there were any letters for his mother. Then he planned to buy the food at the market. Roberto set off with a shopping list for the warehouse of Ling Pa. They arranged to meet later at the landing stage, where the boat lay.

Ling Pa's store was full of people. Roberto had to wait a long time. César Gomez entered. Ignoring the waiting line, he gave his orders. Roberto watched him furtively. He remembered Pedro's story. Though the son was not responsible for the father's deeds, it did throw a different light on Gomez in Roberto's eyes.

"What do you want?" a shop assistant asked him with a bored face.

Roberto handed him the paper with the shopping list. Without hurrying, the assistant began to gather the items together.

Roberto sauntered through the store till he got to the end where the sacks of beans and flour were. The sacks were stacked to the ceiling. Between them narrow passages had been left. Even in the daytime it was dark there. Out of boredom Roberto entered one of the passages and peered into the darkness. It's just like a maze, he thought. He was about to turn back when his attention was caught by hushed voices. In the maze between the sacks some men were holding a whispered conversation. Roberto stood stock still and listened.

". . . well thought out."

"Yes, but. . . ."

"But what?"

"No joke . . . through the jungle. . . ."

"Your plan . . . the river . . . too dangerous you said."

"Yes, but. . . ."

"Well. . . ."

"We want more money."

"More money? You're crazy. Not a penny."

There followed a silence. Roberto held his breath. What's this? he thought. What are they talking about? Why are these people hiding here? What kind of mystery is this? Again he heard voices, much lower now.

". . . don't want to be discovered . . . great detour . . . over Red Lake . . . do you know what that means? Dangerous . . . more money."

"You're a villain . . . the arrangement is. . . ."

"Tut, tut, your weapons. . . ."

Roberto's breath caught. Weapons! He had heard the word very clearly. Were they weapon smugglers, those people a few yards away? They must be! Who were they?

Roberto crept cautiously farther through the passage. It was too dark to distinguish anything. Yet those men must be very near. Perhaps in one of the cross aisles. Again Roberto took a step forward. His shoulder hit a flour bag. A white cloud puffed out and filled his nostrils.

"Ha . . . tchoo!" sneezed Roberto. "Hatchoo! Hatchoo!" The talk immediately stopped. He heard a slight noise. Those horrible bags . . . that rotten flour . . . thought Roberto. Hatchoo, hatchooo hatchoo!

He could spare himself any further trouble. Everyone in the store knew where he was now. He shuffled back and was grabbed roughly by the neck and pulled away from the sacks.

"You young snot nose," said a voice, trembling with rage. Roberto looked straight into the face of Ling Pa.

"Aha, Mr. Roberto," he barked. " I thought you'd be spying about here."

"But I . . . ." said Roberto, dismayed.

"You need not tell me anything different, friend," spat Ling Pa. "It isn't the first time that you've stuck your nose into my affairs. I'm warning you. If I see you set foot into my store again, I'll. . . ."

But Roberto did not wait to hear what Ling Pa would do. He tore himself loose and ran out of the warehouse. He ran on and on till he reached the pier. Trembling, dripping with sweat, he stopped and looked around.

Where is Felipe? I must tell him at once what I've

heard. We must let Don Luís know immediately, he thought. But he did not see Felipe nor did he see the motorboat with Alvaro.

"Are you looking for someone?" asked a dirty little shoeshine boy.

"Have you seen a motorboat with a man and a boy in it? They were going to wait here."

The shoeshine boy grinned mischievously. "I've seen them," he said. "If you're quick, you can see them too. There they go . . . in the distance!"

Roberto peered across the water. It was true. Far away the little motorboat was disappearing in the direction of La Bocana. In it Roberto saw Felipe and Alvaro and a third person who looked like Don Luís. Roberto grew pale with anger. He left the landing stage.

"What a mean trick to leave me behind here!" he growled.

"Well, Roberto, is something wrong?"

Roberto looked around. Old Josué sat on a bench. "Good morning, Josué. I didn't know you had put in," said Roberto. "How are you?"

"I'm all right, but you look as if you're upset about something."

"I should say so!" cried Roberto. "Felipe was supposed to wait here and take me back in the boat to La Bocana. But he's gone off and left me standing here with the groceries." At that moment Roberto discovered that he did not have the groceries after all! Old Josué saw that he did not too. They both grinned.

"I mean," said Roberto, "that I went to Ling Pa's store to buy groceries but I forgot all about them when they chased me out."

"Chased you?" echoed old Josué.

"Yes, when I stood in the warehouse I heard such a strange conversation! I think it was about smuggling weapons." Roberto bent toward old Josué and whispered, "I know how they're smuggling the weapons. Through the jungle."

"The jungle!" said Josué. "Roberto, are you sure?" When Roberto nodded, the old man added slowly, "That's scarcely possible."

"It's true. I heard them say so," said Roberto. "They even mentioned the place. They're going across Red Lake. Did you ever hear of it?"

"Yes," said old Josué slowly. "Yes, I've heard of it. But if that's true, then. . . ." He did not finish his sentence and stared across the water.

"Well," insisted Roberto. "What do you think?"

Old Josué remained silent, staring ahead reflectively. "The jungle and Red Lake," he repeated. "That's a dangerous undertaking. It's nearly impossible."

"But I heard the words clearly," said Roberto. In his voice sounded all the pride of having made an important discovery. He looked across the bay at the distant jungle. "I'd like to see that place," he muttered.

He remained staring at the far shore, where the trees were wrapped in a blue-green haze. Lonely, mysterious, deserted, and beguiling, there lay the vast jungle.

Josué regarded Roberto silently. Did the old man see the longing for adventure in the boy's eyes? "I warn you," he said. "If you really want to go into the jungle, do not go alone. It's dangerous. Not only because of smugglers, the jungle itself is dangerous. The *selvas bravas* are wild woods. Certainly for an inexperienced boy."

"I wanted to tell Felipe and Don Luís what I heard," said Roberto ruefully. "But they've left me stranded here."

"You heard what I said," said old Josué. He got up slowly. But Roberto would not let him go.

"Josué," he said quickly. "Do you know where Red Lake is? Can you get a canoe?"

Old Josué looked back at him. "Do you really want to go then?" he asked.

"Yes," answered Roberto firmly. Felipe and Don Luís can go chase themselves, he thought resentfully. I'll teach them to leave me standing here like a fool!

"Come along then," said Old Josué. "The tide is rising. Now is the best time to enter the jungle."

Trembling with eagerness, Roberto ran behind old Josué. At the pile dwellings near the shore, on the half-inundated silt stretch, Josué entered one of the hovels. He exchanged a few words with an old crone, crouching on the floor there. A moment later he rejoined Roberto, who had remained standing under the rickety ladder.

"It's all right," he said.

He pulled a canoe from under the hut and shoved it far into the water. "Step in," he said. Then he pushed a second canoe into the water, which he entered himself.

"What are you doing?" asked Roberto.

"I told you, didn't I, that you can't go alone into the jungle?" grumbled Josué. He poled his canoe into deep water. Silently they crossed the broad river.

10

THE RED LAKE

They slid into the jungle. The sunlight filtered through the heavy leaves and made fitful patterns on the dark water. There was a green smell. The roots of the high trees were planted broadly in the water. The air roots of the mangroves twisted together like lean, brown fingers.

The open water between the trees became narrower.

The shrubbery thrust itself more and more forward. The two canoes paddled single file into a narrow creek.

It was very still. The sounds of the outside world did not penetrate here. Now and then a leaf fell, rustling through the branches, a little fish flipped out of the water, a bird screamed. There was no other sound.

Regularly the paddles swished through the water. Old Josué was in front. Roberto imitated all his motions. For a long time they continued that way—the old man and the boy—wordlessly, each absorbed in his own thoughts. Old Josué looked neither up nor down. With long, powerful strokes he propelled his canoe forward in the narrow creek between the high rushes. Roberto sometimes had difficulty keeping up with him.

Old Josué's canoe slid around a bend of the creek out of sight. For a moment Roberto had the eerie feeling of being the only person on earth, the only one in this deserted, green world. Then his canoe also rounded the bend, and he saw Josué again.

The creek branched many times. They crossed hundreds of other narrow creeks and rivers. They were paddling through a maze of smaller and larger waterways.

As old Josué had said, the tide was coming in. The water rose higher and higher over the brownish roots of the mangroves and the trunks of the trees. Peering between the green leaves and branches, Roberto saw the water glitter far off in the wilderness.

For the first few hours he did not tire, but then

paddling became a burden. They went up a little river. The sun beat down fiercely on the water, and it reflected the heat. On the narrow creeks, between the thick green, it had been stifling hot, but shaded. Here Roberto was blinded by the sparkling surface of the water. The sun shone directly on his head. Sweat poured over his face. He had a raging thirst and was dead tired. He lagged farther and farther behind.

Old Josué looked back. "What's the matter?" he asked.

"I'm thirsty, and I don't seem to make headway anymore."

Old Josué pointed to the water circling sluggishly between the tree trunks. "That's because the tide is changing," he said. "The flood has reached its highest point; the water has halted. If we want to reach Red Lake before low tide, we have to get a move on."

The river branched off several times. Again they entered the damp, twilight forest. They paddled along shores with ferns yards high, the fronds bent like feathers over the narrow creeks. From the heavy trees climbing plants hung down like green tears.

Then the woods opened, and the two canoes entered a small lake. It was not so much a lake as a meeting place of rivulets and creeks, broad and narrow, which flowed together here to separate again and continue their course through the vast jungle. It was a silent pool of water with deep inlets and far jutting spits of land, grown over with high reeds and papyrus plants.

Hundreds of water birds floated on the mirroring water.

Wading birds paddled along the shoreline. The bottom of the lake had a reddish brown color, which gave the water a rosy tint. The lake lay like a little pink pearl in the mighty green fist of the forest.

A flight of small wild ducks, roused by the canoes, took off from the water. A blue heron winged its way to the opposite shore.

They crossed the lake, going past many spits of land. At last Old Josué found a narrow inlet, lined with waving rushes, which seemed suitable to him. He entered it and stuck his paddle beside the canoe into the soft ground. Roberto came alongside.

"Here we are then," said Old Josué, looking about him. Roberto wiped his face with his arm. "I'm thirsty," he said.

Old Josué bent down. At the bottom of the canoe, between his feet, lay a bottle. He handed it to Roberto. "Have a drink," he said.

Gladly Roberto put the bottle to his lips and drank. Making a grimace, he returned the bottle quickly. "It's *aguardiente*. I thought it was water," he said.

"Water!" growled old Josué contemptuously. "You don't think I'd bother to carry water! I see enough of that!" He put the bottle to his lips and drank lustily.

Roberto said nothing. The sharp taste of anise still burned his tongue and his throat. His thirst had not been quenched.

The sun was losing its force. In the moderate light clouds of mosquitoes arose above the reedy shores. They hummed around Roberto's head and stung him horribly. Rapidly it became dark. A gray mist rose from the lake and mingled with the deep purple shadows of the forest. It was very still.

Roberto looked around. The night shadows crept nearer and nearer over the water, out of the rushes, out of the forest. "Must . . . must we stay here all night?" he asked.

Old Josué shrugged his shoulders. "You wanted to come," he said. "If you want to surprise smugglers, you must have patience. Besides, it's too late to go back now." He stared over the water.

"I must say," he said after a while, "that those fellows made a good choice. You can escape from here in all directions." He nodded approvingly and took a big swallow of *aguardiente*. He handed Roberto the bottle again. "If I were you, I'd have another drink," he said. "It's cold on the water at night. You'd better fortify yourself. *Aguardiente* is good against the cold."

Roberto dared not refuse. He was shivering already. Not from cold, but from apprehension. In the morning, in the town, with the sun on the water and the jungle miles away, it had seemed a very adventurous idea to spy on the smugglers. But with the disappearance of the daylight the romance seemed to have disappeared too. Roberto now wished he had never started this trip. He suddenly remembered Emperatriz's story of the five men who had gone into the jungle and had never returned. A shiver ran down his back.

"Cold?" asked old Josué. He took another swallow.

"No, I'm not cold. But . . . did you ever hear about five men who wanted to shoot wild duck here in the jungle and . . . and who were never heard of again? Perhaps they were here, on this very lake. . . ."

Old Josué shrugged his shoulders. "I don't know," he said. "It could be. . . ."

They sat silently and stared into the gloaming. Roberto had to acknowledge that the *aguardiente* helped. He did not shiver anymore, and he began to feel calmer. He was still thirsty, and when old Josué handed him the bottle again he took two long draughts.

"Good," said old Josué. "You're learning. When I was your age, I drank like a man. How do you think I could have survived otherwise?"

Roberto did not answer. He couldn't imagine the rough, miserable life that Josué had led as a boy on board the dirty old freighters. Silently they sat together.

Somewhere a branch snapped and a bird flew screeching out of the long rushes. It startled them. Sharply they listened, but all remained still.

"I thought for a moment they were coming," whispered Roberto.

"Yes," said old Josué in a low voice. A moment later he added, "Roberto, we are not very clever to remain together in the same place. You never know. . . . If they spot us, they catch two flies with one slap. Why don't I go to the opposite shore? Then we can guard the lake from two sides."

"But . . . but . . . must I stay here alone?" asked Roberto, frightened.

"Yes, that can't be helped. Anyway it's a small lake. If you call, I'll hear you at once. You must only take care not to betray your presence to the smugglers. A voice carries far over the water."

"Yes," said Roberto. He did not like to remain alone, but old Josué was right. If the smugglers should catch them together, they were powerless.

Cautiously old Josué pulled his paddle out of the mud. Silently he guided his canoe out of the inlet.

Roberto saw him slide away over the water and disappear into the misty darkness. He remained sitting, silent and alone.

Now he began to notice how tired he was. His arms ached, and he felt stiff from sitting so long in the same cramped position. The mosquito bites itched, and he still was terribly thirsty. It seemed as if the *aguardiente* had made his throat still dryer. His head hummed. He shifted his position. He stared at the sky. Above the forest twinkled the stars. The night wind stirred the water. The reeds rustled. Or was it the wind?

A vague unrest came over him. A feeling of approaching disaster. Sharply he listened. Again something rustled. Did he hear a sound on the water? Should he call Josué? But if it was the smugglers he'd betray himself. Roberto could not bear the tension anymore. Against his better judgment he called.

"Josué! Josué!"

"Yes," Josué answered. "What's the matter?"

"Nothing," said Roberto.

"Then hold your tongue, damn it!"

Roberto felt unbelievably stupid. There was nothing to be afraid of. Old Josué lay at the opposite shore not far away. They were both well hidden. They would hear at once if the smugglers entered the lake. Perhaps they'd even be able to see them. They were prepared; the smugglers didn't know they were lying in wait for them, at least if he, Roberto, didn't warn them with his stupid calling. If he remained sensible and didn't let fear sweep over him, nothing could happen.

Roberto changed his position once more. He rested his elbows on his knees and put his chin on his hands. He kept staring at the sky. Thick clouds came floating and the little twinkling stars disappeared one by one behind them. But Roberto did not see them anymore. . . .

11

SELVAS BRAVAS

Roberto awoke with a start, because the rain came streaming down on him. The night was gray. The rain shot arrows into the lake, pitting the black surface. A moment later Roberto was drenched.

Hunching his shoulders together, he sat there. There was no point in seeking shelter. The rain rustled through the reed stalks. The trees dripped. But he dared not leave his canoe. His teeth chattered with the cold. Everywhere was the sound of rain: in the forest, on the lake, in the rushes.

The water drummed into the canoe. His feet were soaking wet. Little streams of it poured down his neck over his back. Water kept gushing out of the clouds. Rustling rain filled the silence of the night for hours on end. At last, toward daybreak, the weather cleared.

Roberto took off his shirt, wrung it dry, and put it on again. He felt miserable—cold, clammy, and stiff. He was tired, hungry, and thirsty. Finally, he decided to look for old Josué.

It wasn't quite light yet. A gray mist swept raggedly over the silent lake. Its shores were hidden from sight. Roberto paddled his canoe out of the inlet with some difficulty. The bottom scraped several times along the ground. Here and there clumps of grass stuck out of the water. It was ebb tide; he must be careful not to get stuck. Cautiously he paddled on. Now that the water was low the lake looked different. Spits of land loomed in the mist.

"Josué," cried Roberto.

His voice sounded muted in the waterlogged air. He got no answer. Carefully Roberto paddled around the spits of land. He tried to peer through the mists into the inlets. The reeds stood motionless. It was still as death.

"Josué!" called Roberto once more. And then he shouted as hard as he could, "*Josué! Where are you*?"

But it remained still. Just in front of his canoe a bird fluttered up from the water, startling him. "Wretched bird," he muttered, annoyed. Then he called once more, "*Josué, Josué*!"

He listened, tense.

Nothing.

Why doesn't he answer? thought Roberto. He must be nearby, in one of these inlets. Perhaps he, like Roberto, had fallen asleep. He had to smile at that thought. It was a normal thing to happen to him, but he could not imagine it of old Josué. Falling asleep wasn't like him. Roberto's face darkened again. Even if he had fallen asleep, Roberto's calling should have wakened him. Why then didn't he answer?

Roberto turned the canoe and paddled back past the many deep and shallow inlets, which his eyes could not penetrate.

"*Josué*!" he called at each inlet. "*Are you there, Josué*!" It began to rain again. Thick drops splashed into the water and ticked the broad leaves of the water plants. Visibility became worse and worse.

Disheartened, Roberto went across the lake, in the streaming rain, past spits of land with dripping reeds, past fog-filled inlets. He could not distinguish the mouths of the creeks and rivers. He saw no sign of old Josué.

But this is impossible, thought Roberto, despairing. "He *must* be here!"

Once more he paddled around the lake, his thoughts crowding wildly in his head.

What could have happened in the night while he slept? Had old Josué discovered the smugglers and followed them? Why hadn't he given a warning then? Maybe there hadn't been time. Maybe the smugglers had surprised him when he was napping in the canoe. No, that wasn't likely. Old Josué wasn't the sort of man who lets himself be taken by surprise. But . . . he was not young anymore . . . and he had been drinking quite a lot the evening before. He'd taken the bottle with him when he went off. Perhaps he had finished it alone. Perhaps he had made an unexpected movement in the dark. Perhaps the canoe had capsized . . . and old Josué had drowned!

Then I am alone, was the thought that flashed through Roberto. Alone in the jungle! But that was impossible!

"No, no," he cried, and saw something floating in front of him that looked like an overturned canoe. The paddle trembled in his hand, and he had almost no strength in his arms as he went to it. The bow of his canoe shoved into a field of floating water hyacinths. Roberto sighed with relief and gave a bad-tempered whack at the tightly matted plants. They separated and drifted off like miniature islands.

But the thought that old Josué had met with an accident would not leave him.

Nervously he recrossed the lake. He searched. He called. There was nothing. No one answered him. The rain stopped. The clouds parted. It became lighter. The sun broke through, and the world around Roberto began to steam. Along the shores the contours of the jungle became visible, but the trees had no substance; they floated on a mist.

Roberto paddled to the shore. He entered an inlet and stuck his paddle in the ground. He sat there, his shoulders hunched together. The sun warmed his back. His clothes dried.

Now I must think clearly and logically, Roberto said to himself. In all likelihood Josué saw the smugglers last night. He has followed them or has gone for help. If so, he'll be back in a few hours to fetch me. And if not. . . . He wiped his forehead with his hand. But the somber thoughts would not leave him. He kept worrying. It *was* possible that the smugglers had discovered Josué and had attacked him. Yet then Roberto would surely have noticed something. If Josué had fallen into the water, he would have known too. Or had he slept so deeply that he hadn't heard the cries of the old man?

"It isn't possible. It simply isn't possible," the boy muttered. Old Josué must have followed the smugglers to see where they went. Then he'd get help and come back to Red Lake. Perhaps he would come with Don Luís, perhaps even with Felipe. How Felipe would hate to have missed this adventure!

Roberto began to feel better.

He took off his sodden shoes, put his paddle across the gunnels of the canoe, and placed his shoes on the blade to dry. Then he got out of the canoe and waded ashore. With some trouble he pushed his way through the reeds and the high grass. At the edge of the jungle he cut, after fumbling a bit, into a climbing plant with his pocketknife and let the juice run into his mouth. He drank greedily. Though he was still hungry, he felt a lot better. He walked back to the canoe. There he found a fallen tree and picked off a piece of the bark. Then he began to scoop the water out of the bottom of the canoe.

When he finished, he put his half-dry shoes inside, picked up his paddle, and reentered the lake.

The mist had dissolved; the inlets were now easily visible. As he rounded each point of land his glance slid swiftly over the water. At each bend hope flashed that he would see Josué sitting quietly in his canoe, and each time he was again disappointed. Along the lakeshore, half-hidden by the reeds, stood great white and blue herons. From time to time they bent their long necks. Their sharp bills pierced the water and speared little fish. Greedily the herons swallowed them. Little wading birds stirred the leaves of the water plants, picking up insects and larvae. Wild ducks searched for food in the water, trying to grab one another's tidbits. The lake dwellers were busy with their breakfasts. Roberto looked quickly away.

He went up a narrow, winding creek. Sunlight sieved through the branches and made playful reflections on the water. Farther on it became dark and chilly. Roberto dared not continue. He was afraid of losing his way, for the creek branched off constantly. He was also afraid that old Josué might come to the lake and find him gone. So he paddled back.

It was probably near noon, for the water had risen considerably. Roberto wandered over the lake. The afternoon seemed endless. Hardly noticeably, the water began to fall again.

No one came.

The sun was cooling. The sky reddened. The brilliant colors of the setting sun were mirrored in the lake. A red glow lay on the water. Herons winged off. Darkness was falling. The mosquitoes started their attack again.

Again Roberto entered an inlet and brought his canoe to rest between the reeds. He looked at the rain forest rising just behind the pale reeds. The high old trees, growing tightly together, filled with black shadows. He did not dare leave his canoe to drink again. He was afraid of possible snakes, which he would not be able to see in time to avoid them in this shadowy world. He was afraid of the dark threat of the rain forest itself. So he decided to try the lake water. He scooped up some with his hand. It was not as salty as he had feared. He quenched his thirst, but he was so hungry that his stomach ached.

And no one came.

Motionless the jungle ringed the lake, the lonely Red Lake, that was no bigger than the size of a pinhead in the vast primeval rain forest on Colombia's western coast.

The short twilight melted into darkness, the darkness of a tropical night. And it began to rain again. Cold, hungry, miserable, Roberto sat in his canoe. He could not sleep, and the night lasted forever. All sorts of things crossed his mind. Sometimes he thought he heard voices or the sound of a paddle in the water. Then again he was certain that old Josué had had an accident. He thought of the conversation he had heard in Ling Pa's shop and of Ling Pa's anger, of Felipe, who had not waited for him. And again he thought of old Josué. Tomorrow he'd be sure to come or to send someone to fetch him. Tomorrow. . . .

The next day started radiantly. The sun glittered on the water, and the dewdrops on plants and bushes shone like brilliants. Hundreds of birds floated like small, dark flakes over the water. It became stifling hot.

Roberto went to and fro across the lake. He listened to each sound. A leaf fell hissing down, a branch creaked, a bird fluttered up. Otherwise, it was still, still and hot. No one came.

The day went by, and the evening fell. A white mist rose from the water. Aimlessly Roberto let his canoe drift. He was now convinced that Josué had had an accident . . . or that the smugglers had got him . . . or that something else had happened. What was it that Emperatriz had said about the five men who had disappeared into the jungle? "It was as if the mists that hovered between the trees had dissolved them." Roberto stared over the lake. Shreds of fog drifted over the water. White shadows moved along the shores. Formless beings, they wandered in silence. Their chill breath moved over the water plants and the rushes, blotting them out, and then they were swallowed up in the brooding darkness of the jungle.

Perhaps, thought Roberto as he stared into the gray gloaming, perhaps Emperatriz is right.

A cold tremor rippled down his back. Hastily he paddled to the shore to a small, protective inlet. He slept for a few hours, but the rain woke him again. It rained for a long time uninterruptedly.

A new morning dawned. He decided to leave the lake and try to find his way back. He waited for high tide. Then he left the little lake, where the sun glittered, and entered the dark jungle.

Roberto felt sure the creek was the same one along which Josué had led him. But after a while he wasn't so sure anymore. He let his paddle rest on the gunwale and looked around. Was it the same one? The creek was narrow. Plants with great spotted and veined leaves and enormous ferns drooped over the dark water. From the trees hung many climbing plants. Was this creek narrower or did it only seem so?

Should he go back to the lake and try again? That would take time, and perhaps this *was* the right creek. When he followed Josué, he hadn't paid much attention; the surroundings were all so similar. He paddled on. The creek branched out, and Roberto chose, after some hesitation, the broader arm of the two. He was going in the right direction anyway. But the narrow, dark creek wound in such a corkscrew fashion through the rain forest that Roberto lost his sense of direction after a while. His canoe slid under slender ferns, past enormous trees, their crowns lost in the green dome above him.

Somewhere in the moist green twilight something white glowed. When Roberto came closer, he saw a cluster of white fleshy orchids on a tree trunk, transparent as the hand of a corpse.

Hastily he went on.

Again the creek branched; again he chose haphazardly. He paddled more slowly. His back ached, the palms of his hands burned, his arms felt like lead. He was dead tired and weak with hunger. To fill his stomach, he drank a lot of the lukewarm brown water in the different creeks. He did not want to open climbing plants with his pocketknife anymore, though he knew their juice was cooler and purer. He did not care anymore. He kept on paddling, along creeks and rivers, past trees, bushes, ferns. Everything was green . . . green . . . a high, almost impenetrable wall of green. And there was silence, the silence of the jungle, a silence trembling with unknown and incomprehensible sounds. He went on.

Then the woods opened, and he entered a drowned world of papyrus and sodden grass. Trees and bushes were strewn about in the water. Branches dipped into it, obstructing his view. Roberto bent and peered ahead. Here, there, everywhere, as far as he could see, water glittered between the slimy air roots, low-hanging branches, and forests of yellow reeds.

He had no idea where he was. He did not know in

[illegible]ection to move anymore, nor did he care. Of course, he would like to leave this lonely, sinister jungle, this deserted, drowned world, but he did not want to go searching for a way out anymore. He was completely exhausted. In four days he had scarcely eaten anything. He was spent, worn out. He had lost heart.

The jungle, the endless, mysterious jungle, had slowly got him in its grasp.

Listlessly he paddled on. Then his canoe hit something under the water and stuck fast. He milled around it with his paddle without success. He grabbed at overhanging branches, to pull himself loose, but they broke. Once more he tried to get free with his paddle, but it slid out of his hand. As he bent to pick it up the mirror image of trees and bushes in the water moved and flowed together. When he straightened, the trees and bushes went on flowing before his eyes, until he could see nothing, nothing at all.

Roberto slumped forward in the canoe. When he regained consciousness, he looked around in surprise. He did not know how long he had been unconscious, but in that time the world around him had changed.

The canoe lay among wet herbs. Reeds, ferns, trees, and bushes stood on undulating ground. Nowhere did he see any water. He gazed, astonished. How had he got here, on dry land, among plants and bushes? Slowly he realized that he had paddled into a swamp during high tide. When the tide turned, the water had receded and the morass had dried up.

Once more Roberto scrutinized his surroundings. His glance fell on the ground.

In the marshy soil just in front of the canoe he saw the imprint of a naked foot.

12

SOJOURN IN THE JUNGLE

It began to darken in between the trees of the rain forest. The shadows crept sluggishly across the marshy ground. They reached out toward the small canoe between the rushes and ferns. But Roberto did not notice. Dazed, he stared at the print beside the canoe. The print of a human foot.

Someone must have been here. Someone had stood next to the canoe and had looked down on him. Who?

Josué, thought Roberto. It must have been Josué. But how was that possible? He had been paddling for hours away from Red Lake. How could Josué have found him here, and why hadn't he stayed? The smugglers! The answer flashed through his mind. Had the smugglers discovered him? Then another awful thought came to him. That one man! The one surviving hunter whom they had seen roaming naked and white through the rain forest. The man who had lost his wits! Roberto felt himself grow cold. His clammy hands clutched the sides of his canoe.

I must get away, he thought. I must get away before the man returns.

He raised himself, lifted his foot over the side of the canoe and put it on the ground. It sank deep into the marshy soil. Again he tried, getting out on the other side. Again his feet sank, deeper at every step. The soft ground sucked at his ankles. Roberto looked back at his canoe. With an effort he pulled his feet loose one by one and slushed back to the canoe. There was no alternative. He would have to wait in his canoe till the flood came. How long would that be?

What would happen to him if that man reappeared? A degenerated, witless man? Roberto looked around anxiously. He noticed how dark it had become. Did something move? Did he hear something? A leaf fluttered down. Silence.

And yet it wasn't completely still. The ground vibrated; the reeds stirred. He was not alone anymore. Instinctively he felt the approach of another creature.

Every fiber in his body tensed. He listened, listened. Glancing rapidly around, he tried to pierce the blue shadows between the reeds with his eyes. Did he see something there? A white spot? A white spot approaching and gaining form. . . .

A face. A gray, emaciated face with burning eyes. Roberto looked dazed into that face, into those eyes. Eyes glittering like those of a hunted animal.

Hoarsely he whispered, "Ordulio!" He scrambled up and held out his hand. Ordulio did not move. Only when Roberto made a motion as if to get out of his canoe did Ordulio make a warning gesture.

"Not there," he said. His voice sounded raspy. "Come to the bow of the canoe. I'll show you where you can stand."

Silently Roberto did as Ordulio told him. A moment later they faced each other among the reeds. Roberto began to tremble so violently that he had to grab hold of Ordulio. "Ordulio . . . you . . . oh, Ordulio. . . . What must I do?"

Ordulio looked down on the boy. He did not say anything. He pushed away Roberto's hand, bent down, and pulled the canoe into the reeds. He tethered the little vessel, looked for the paddle and put it inside. Without a glance at Roberto, he turned and said, "Come along." They walked single file into the swamp. With unerring certainty Ordulio followed an invisible path, which twisted and turned between reeds, ferns, shrubs, and water plants. Roberto walked right behind Ordulio. Automatically he imitated every movement, every step of his guide.

It darkened more and more. At last they came to a border of high shrubbery. When they pushed through the bushes, Roberto noticed that the ground was firmer here and sloped upward. They reached a little open place.

"Here it is," said Ordulio.

Roberto could discern faintly a little hut. It was not more really than a lean-to of palm leaves. Roberto threw himself down on the trampled ground in front of the hut.

"Are you hungry?"

Roberto nodded. "Yes!" he said wearily.

Ordulio disappeared into the darkness at the side of the hut. A moment later he returned with some fish and wild papaya fruit. He handed the food to Roberto in a freshly picked leaf. Roberto fell on it. The fish was half raw, but he scarcely noticed. He also devoured the unripe papaya greedily.

Ordulio had seated himself under the lean-to and seemed to be staring at Roberto. It had now become quite dark. The sky was sprinkled with stars, and above the jungle trees the moon rose. Roberto now joined Ordulio inside the lean-to. He lay quietly beside him, listening to the sounds of the night. Insects hummed, crickets chirped, and far in the depths of the wilderness an animal screeched. At the edge of the swamp the crowns of the trees were silhouetted against the moonlit sky. Not a leaf stirred around the hut, but down at the swamp the reeds rustled and between the ferns and water plants something murmured and whispered.

"What's that?" asked Roberto.

"The tide is rising."

"Oh," said Roberto with a sigh.

The water crept steadily higher in the swamp. But he lay dry and comfortable in the little hut. He was tired, exhausted, and grateful to Ordulio for not speaking, not asking questions. He could not have told what he had suffered: the fear, the hunger, the despair, the terrible loneliness.

Now he was no longer alone. Ordulio was with him. Ordulio . . . an escaped murderer. . . .

The sky clouded, and it began to rain hard. While the water drummed on the leafy roof of the lean-to, Roberto fell into a fitful sleep.

When he awoke the next morning, he was alone in the hut. He crawled from under the lean-to and observed his surroundings. A little fire smoldered in a hole in the ground. Around it lay some gnawed bones and the remains of some fish. Ordulio was nowhere to be seen.

"Ordulio!" cried Roberto. No one answered. His voice died away in the silence. A despairing fear came over him. Was he alone again? Had Ordulio disappeared like Josué? But he did not want to be alone anymore. He wanted to get away, away from the jungle. He stormed down the hill. Hacking his way through the bushes, he ran blindly into the swamp. His feet sank down in the marshy bottom. He pulled himself loose; he stumbled on. His feet sank deeper, air bubbles welled up, the mud sucked at his ankles. He grabbed the branches of a bush.

"Ordulio, Ordulio!" he yelled.

The bushes moved. Ordulio peered through the leaves. He glanced around furtively. "What's the matter?" he whispered.

"Oh, Ordulio! I thought you had gone!"

"Gone? Is that all? You're crazy to shout like that."

Roberto's feet were sinking deeper into the bog. Ordulio pulled him up with a jerk onto firm ground. He put his gray, emaciated face close to Roberto's. "Don't you dare shout like that again, or call my name. You could have given me away with that stupid yelling!"

Roberto swallowed a few times. Ordulio turned his back to him and walked away. Roberto followed him mutely to the hut.

Ordulio began to tend the fire. Roberto sat down beside him. After a while he said, "Where were you?"

"I went to get the canoe. I left while it was still ebb tide, and when the water rose I paddled here."

"Oh," said Roberto. Now that he could think clearly again he understood why Ordulio had been angry. He looked at Ordulio out of the corner of his eye. Ordulio's face was severe. His lean hands were restless.

"I'm sorry I shouted," said Roberto in a subdued voice. "But I was with old Josué on the lake, and the next day I couldn't find him. I was frightened. It was so lonesome

. . . and the mist. . . . I still don't know what happened to him."

Roberto stopped talking and looked shyly at Ordulio. Ordulio crouched in a hunched position. His hands hung between his bony knees while his lean fingers played with a wisp of straw. He stared at the ground. Was he listening?

Roberto sighed. He hated Ordulio's silence. Once more he tried to get him to talk. "Do you often walk through the swamp? How did you happen to find me?"

Ordulio shrugged his shoulders. "By chance," he said. More to himself than to Roberto, he added, "I always go during low tide to the swamp to look for food. Now I have the canoe it will be easier."

"I'm glad you found me," Roberto said in a low voice. "I was afraid. . . . There was a footprint near my canoe, a human footprint. I thought. . . ." Roberto halted. He looked at Ordulio to see if he could understand without words the terrible thoughts he had had. Ordulio lifted his hand. "I had been there before."

The words hung in the trembling heat. At last Roberto whispered, "You saw me before . . . and went away?" Ordulio gave no answer. Thoughts tumbled in Roberto's head.

Ordulio's footprint was the one that he had seen in the soft swamp bottom. Ordulio had found him and had quietly left him. What had moved him to come back? Had he wanted to get the canoe, or had he been unable to leave him to his fate?

Roberto did not dare ask the question, and probably

Ordulio would not have been able to answer it. By saving Roberto he had betrayed his hiding place to another human being. Did he regret his action? Silently they sat on the little hill, each wrapped in his own thoughts.

At last Roberto fell into an uneasy sleep. He slept at intervals that whole day and the next. When he woke, he ate the fish and wild fruit Ordulio brought him. The jungle provided enough, enough to keep them alive.

The days went by, and Roberto's strength returned. He longed for his home; he wanted to leave the rain forest. But something kept him from speaking about his return. Ordulio did not mention it either.

One morning he lay in the shade of the hut, peering through his eyelashes at Ordulio. Ordulio was sitting near the shrubbery. He was busy making a snare with plant fibers. His head was bent over his work; his long black hair hung untidily over his forehead and shoulders. His lean, dirty fingers pulled the noose of the snare back and forth.

"What are you going to do with that?"

"I'm going to see if I can catch something. I've seen the trail of some little wild pigs, the ones that they call *tabras.*"

"Oh," said Roberto. He followed Ordulio's movements through his eyelashes. How long had Ordulio been living here in the rain forest? How long had he been eating fish and plant roots, hunting game with primitive tools? Did he want to stay here forever?

Ordulio looked up suddenly. Did he feel he was being watched? "What are you looking at?"

"Nothing. I wasn't looking."

Ordulio sniffed and spat on the ground. He got up abruptly. "I'm ready," he said. "The water is rising. Come along."

"What are we going to do?" asked Roberto listlessly.

Ordulio looked him over silently. Then he said, "We have to put out the snares and catch something. You want to eat, don't you?"

Roberto got up unwillingly. Ordulio waited until Roberto had gone into the shrubbery. Then he followed him to the canoe.

They paddled through the swamp. Roberto sat idle in the bow; Ordulio paddled. He had taken possession of the canoe. They slid into the dark, dank jungle. Roberto gazed at the impenetrable rotting greenness. It made him sick. He hated it. I can't stand it here. I want to go home, he thought. Want to go home . . . home . . . home. He turned around impulsively. "What direction are we going?"

"We're going to the place where I saw the tracks of the *tabras.*"

"But is it north or south? Which way is Buenaventura?"

"Buenaventura?" muttered Ordulio. "I'm not interested in Buenaventura." He paddled on, looking grim. Then he said angrily, "Why do you ask that?"

"For no reason," said Roberto hastily. He turned his face away, but he felt that Ordulio was staring at him.

There was tension in the atmosphere. A despairing feeling came over Roberto. The vague anxiety of the last days changed into panic. Loneliness wasn't what he feared now. Why doesn't he give me a straight answer? Doesn't he see how unhappy I am? thought Roberto rebelliously. I can't stand it any longer. I'll have to think of something.

They penetrated deeper and deeper into the jungle. Branches and fern fronds swept against their faces. It was oppressively hot and humid. The thick roof of leaves made by the gigantic trees spread overhead like a somber, eternally green dome.

"They must be here somewhere," Ordulio said at last. He got out of the canoe, pulled it into the bushes, and waited till Roberto had got out too.

They waded through the jungle over their ankles in mud. Gradually the ground became firmer. But the wet leaves of the underbrush soaked their clothes, which were constantly snagged by the sharp thorns of the low branches.

Ordulio stood still so suddenly that Roberto collided with him. Startled, he jumped backward. Ordulio half turned. "I'm only going to put out a snare. If you come along, you may destroy the track. Wait here. I'll be back soon."

Without waiting for an answer, he went on alone. The jungle closed after him. Leaves rustled, branches snapped, then it was still.

Roberto remained behind alone. His breath came

quickly. He was imprisoned on every side by the dense bushes, the close, damp underbrush. Slowly Roberto's eyes examined the wall of greenness. Then he looked back. The path they had made was plainly visible. Leaves trodden, branches broken. . . . For a while he stared at this trail. He'd easily be able to find the place where the canoe was hidden.

Shall I venture it? he thought. Shall I go back to the canoe? And then? What would he do then?

Then at least he'd have the canoe again. Then he. . . .

Roberto took a few steps and halted. He hesitated. Did he dare go alone through the jungle again, seeking a way out? He was rested now. He felt fit, and mentally he was better prepared for what awaited him.

It's my chance, he thought. I'll have to decide. I must go now. It's now or never. . . . His heart beat wildly. Should he do it? Yes! Yes!

Branches parted, and Ordulio appeared. Roberto had hesitated too long. The moment for escape had passed.

13

DAYS OF DOUBTING

They did not catch a *tabra.* On two consecutive days they went to the place where Ordulio had placed his snare. When they walked through the jungle, hope flared in Roberto that Ordulio would ask him to wait again. But Ordulio said nothing, and Roberto could only follow him meekly. The tracks had been washed away. The snare was empty. On the first day they found, near the snare, a bread tree. They picked the great green fruit, and in the evening they cooked them over a fire. They tasted like chestnuts. The second day they passed some guamas. They pulled down the brown beans from the trees and sucked the sweet white flesh from the black pits.

On the way back, in the canoe, Ordulio discovered a chontaduro palm. The slender trunk of this tree is covered with long, sharp needles, and getting at the hard, yellow fruit is troublesome. They cut a long stick of bamboo and made a loop of fibers at its end. They angled it until the loop caught around a bunch of the fruit. Then they pulled with all their might till the bunch fell crashing to the ground.

"Hurry up," said Ordulio, as he threw the bunch of fruit into the canoe. "It's late. When the water goes down, we can't cross the swamp and reach our hut."

"You wanted to pick the chontaduros yourself," said Roberto.

"Of course, and why do you think I want them? Because they're nourishment, because the pips contain oil, because I need more to live on now that you're here."

Roberto was shocked by this outburst, more because of the roughness of Ordulio's tone than because of the words themselves. He looked down at his dirty, scratched hands and said nothing. Silently they went back to their lean-to.

They put the chontaduro fruit on the smoldering fire and covered it with leaves. Then they sat and waited.

After a while Ordulio broke the heavy silence. His

voice was milder, as if he regretted his outburst. "I know a place where there are *rascaderas*. We'll go there tomorrow."

Tomorrow, tomorrow, thought Roberto, despairing. How long would this ordeal continue? What did Ordulio want with him? Did he intend to keep him there forever, so he could have company in the wilderness? What could he do? He felt worried and nervous. It was harder and harder for him to behave normally. And yet, thought Roberto, that is the only way. I can't do anything against Ordulio's will.

"What are *rascaderas*?" he asked.

"Don't you know? They're plants with heart-shaped leaves. The roots are edible, just like potatoes."

Roberto nodded. What do I care? he thought bitterly. What does anything matter?

The next day they went looking for the *rascaderas*. They dug out the roots with their hands, loaded them into the canoe, and brought them to the hut. Ordulio tended the fire and put the roots, wrapped in leaves, in a hole in the ground.

Again they sat in front of the hut. They heard the water gurgle gently out of the swamp. Roberto picked up a stick and scratched aimlessly over the ground with it.

"Hush!"

Roberto stopped, the stick in his lifted hand. He looked at Ordulio, who was listening intently. "What's the matter? Do you hear something?"

"Yes, hush!" Soundlessly Ordulio rose, his eyes fixed on the shrubbery. Now Roberto heard it too, a light rustling.

"It's probably a lizard," he whispered.

Again the rustling came from the shrubbery, now more clearly.

What can it be? thought Roberto. Was somebody there? Had they been discovered? Noiselessly Ordulio crept to the edge of the bushes. Roberto followed him with his eyes. Ordulio looked like a beast of prey, crouched and silent. He peered into the bushes, measured the distance, and leaped.

There was a shrill cry.

Roberto jumped up. With a few steps he reached the shrubbery. Ordulio lay on the ground. He held a big rodent between his hands—a *guagua*. The *guagua* cried with terror. Its hind legs with their sharp nails scratched Ordulio's wrists open.

Ordulio strengthened the grip of his left hand and felt with his right hand for his knife. Then he stabbed. He threw the dead *guagua* into the clearing and crawled out of the shrubbery. In front of the hut he skinned the *guagua*. The warm, red blood ran down his hands.

Roberto watched him silently. Without exactly looking at Ordulio, he did not miss any of his movements. He saw how Ordulio stripped the soft brownish skin slowly from the *guagua*. He saw him shake his long hair impatiently out of his eyes and then brush his bloodstained cheek with his shoulder.

How he has changed, thought Roberto. Nothing was left of the kind, jolly engineer whom Roberto had known. He looked like a savage. He was lean, his face was emaciated, the high cheekbones stuck out. The lank black hair touched his shoulders and hung in his eyes. The expression of the eyes had changed the most. They looked frightened, wild. . . .

He's short-tempered and nervous, thought Roberto. The tension he lives under is making him dangerous. Roberto averted his face. He did not want to admit it, but he had become afraid of Ordulio.

Ordulio threw the skin of the *guagua* at Roberto's feet. "Here, clean it," he ordered. He walked to the fire, shoveled the half-cooked roots out with an impatient movement, and put his prey on a spit.

Roberto got up and walked with the pelt to the swamp. At its edge he stood still, near a rill of turbid water. He sat down on his haunches and saw his canoe lying nearby, under overhanging fern fronds. He looked at it for a long time, and then his eyes took in the swamp from which the water had almost flowed away. There, in the distance, he still saw a gleam of water. If only he could reach it with his canoe! But that was impossible, and anyway how could he ever find his way out of the jungle alone? A few days ago he had thought he could manage. Now he was doubtful again.

Slowly and indifferently Roberto began to rinse the bloody skin of the *guagua*.

The sun sank behind the trees; the sky reddened. The

first purple shadows detached themselves from the woods and crept between the dense reeds, descending under the bushes. Was Roberto imagining things, or did he hear Ordulio? He had a notion that Ordulio scarcely ever let him out of his sight. Did Ordulio know that Roberto was trying to find some means to get away? Again he heard something move, quite near, between the branches. Out of the corner of his eye he peered to see if it was Ordulio. Instead, it was a big snake, which was slowly letting itself down from a branch, right next to Roberto's shoulder.

He dared not move. Hypnotized, he followed the slowly unwinding snake with his eyes.

"Aren't you ready yet? What are you doing?" Ordulio's voice sounded impatient. "I. . . ."

Then he saw the snake and Roberto's fear-distorted face. Searching around him, he grabbed a stick with a forked point from the ground. He waited a moment, till the snake had slid down. Then he stuck the fork of the stick right behind the serpent's head into the soft ground.

For a moment Roberto remained motionless. The long brown body of the snake writhed in a thousand curves and almost reached Roberto's foot. Roberto flew up and leaped away.

Ordulio bent down. With his free hand he grabbed the snake behind the head. His fingers squeezed together. Then he took away the stick and lifted the curving snake's body. The snake's mouth opened, and a slimy, stinking saliva ran out of its mouth over Ordulio's hand.

Ordulio killed the snake and threw it into the swamp. His hands stank terribly, and he washed them in the bog water without results. They went back to their hut.

The evening fell. The full moon rose above the tops of the trees. The pale moonlight fell on the clearing before the hut. Ordulio cut off a piece of the *guagua* with his knife and began to gnaw on it. He sat with spread legs, his elbows on his knees. With his teeth he tore the half-raw meat from the bone. He threw away the bone and sat still, holding his hands away from himself. They still stank. The air was polluted by the snake's saliva. It made Roberto ill, and he moved back a bit.

Ordulio's face betrayed no emotion. He sat as motionless as one in a trance. Roberto watched him covertly. He could not understand Ordulio. Was he thinking of what had happened? What would have become of him if Ordulio had not arrived? Roberto himself would never have had the courage, but Ordulio hadn't hesitated to kill the snake.

He asked, "How did you dare attack that snake?"

Ordulio shrugged his shoulders. "*Petacas* are not poisonous," he said. "They only stink. If I had seen right away that it was a *petaca,* I wouldn't have killed it. They aren't harmful. The blacks say that they hypnotize the birds with the stench from their mouth. Now I'm stuck with it. I won't get that smell off my hands for a long time."

Roberto reflected on Ordulio's words. He felt confused. Ordulio is sorry he killed the snake, because his hands smell bad, he thought. But when he imagined I was in danger, he grabbed it without hesitating. Ordulio had come to his aid for the second time. And still Robert distrusted him.

"I won't be able to make a snare for several days," said Ordulio.

"Are you going to stay in the jungle for a long time?" Roberto spoke without thinking. Ordulio lifted his head. He looked at Roberto, and their eyes met.

"I don't know. I can't leave for a while. Because of the weapons smuggling Buenaventura is watched twice as carefully. You know that the police are looking for me?"

Roberto nodded. "Why did you do it?" he asked. The moment the words slipped out he regretted them.

Ordulio rubbed his forehead. "A family matter," he muttered. "He was a bad one. One evening he was hanging around our house again. When I told him that my sister wanted to have nothing to do with him and that he'd better go, he attacked me. It was his life or mine."

It was still for a moment. Then he added, "I'm fairly safe here. No one will seek me in the jungle, at least if you don't betray me."

"I!" said Roberto. "I'll never betray you. You saved my life. If you hadn't pulled me out of the swamp to your hut. . . ."

Ordulio laughed scornfully. "That's what you think now," he said. "But when you're safely home, you'll change your mind. In the eyes of your family and the rest of the world I'm a criminal."

"But you saved me," said Roberto again.

"It won't make any difference to the police," Ordulio interrupted him. "Even if you don't give information on purpose, you could easily say something. . . . " Ordulio suddenly stopped talking. In the bright moonlight they looked at each other as if to read each other's mind, plumb each other's emotions.

"What are you going to do?" whispered Roberto.

Ordulio remained silent.

Each was lost in his own thoughts. Would Roberto betray Ordulio if he got the chance? Was Ordulio sorry that he hadn't left Roberto to his fate in the swamp?

Could Roberto keep his mouth shut?

Would Ordulio ever let him go voluntarily?

Roberto said hoarsely, "I'll never betray you, but I want to go home."

"I'll show you the way," said Ordulio. "Tonight."

A heavy load seemed to fall from Roberto's shoulders.

14

A DISCOVERY

They waited till high tide. Then the two of them shoved the canoe down the hill. Roberto sat in front; Ordulio took the paddle and pushed the canoe away from the shore. They slid through the reeds. The moon lit up the deserted swamp. In the pale light it had the unreal appearance of a landscape on another planet. The reed stalks gleamed, and under the broad leaves of the water plants lay deep, dark shadows. Slender fern leaves were etched like gigantic feathers against the silver sky. Moonlight sifted through the delicate leaf patterns.

The canoe scraped over a shallow place in the swamp and stuck. Roberto began to worry that it might get hopelessly caught, but together they pulled it afloat again. At last they entered an open, navigable channel, bordered by rushes. Though Roberto had traversed the marshes with Ordulio for many days, he did not know this place at all. The channel curved through a field of reeds. The moonlight drew a pale trail in the water.

"Ordulio," whispered Roberto. "Where are we?"

But Ordulio did not answer. He paddled silently on. They approached the edge of the jungle. Like an impenetrable black wall the age-old trees rose before them. Roberto caught sight of a high, white figure with outstretched arms, barring their way. He gave a yell of fear.

"What's the matter?" asked Ordulio, throwing a frightened glance around him.

"There, that figure! Oh, Ordulio, what is it?"

"A dead tree, idiot. If you open your mouth once more, I'm going back."

The canoe now slid past the dead tree, which was standing far out in the water. It was only a naked, smooth trunk with a few stunted branches, blanched by sun and rain, on which the moon shone brightly. They paddled into the darkness of the jungle, between the enormous black tree roots, roots that sank deeply into the shadowed water.

From the field of rushes they had just left came a voice. It said, "Did you hear that?"

"What?"

"A . . . well, it sounded like a yell."

"It was a bird probably."

"But. . . ."

"Oh, keep quiet."

With a quick movement Ordulio grabbed a low branch. He pulled the canoe between the air roots of a tree, in the deep shadow of the overhanging leaves. Petrified they sat there and peered between the twigs.

Out of the swamp gray forms detached themselves. From the channel between the reeds a row of canoes approached. Four canoes. They lay deep in the water. In each canoe sat two people. One after the other they disappeared into the jungle.

The procession went so silently and swiftly that Roberto dared not believe his eyes. "Ordulio," he whispered. "Did you see that?"

"Hold your tongue," snarled Ordulio. He swore softly.

Roberto clenched his teeth for fear Ordulio would hear them chatter. He was frightened by the sudden appearance of the canoes. He was afraid that Ordulio would turn back. Breathlessly he waited. What would Ordulio do?

Quietly Ordulio set his canoe in motion again. They

slid from under the overhanging branches and went deeper into the jungle. Roberto noticed that they had entered a narrow creek. It was pitch dark. Almost without transition, the high trees separated abruptly, and the moonlight gleamed on the broad leaves of banana plants. Ordulio paddled to the shore.

In a low voice he said, "I dare go no farther. Do you know where you are?"

Roberto hesitated a moment. He got out of the canoe and scrambled ashore.

"The banana plantation of Manuel el Bobo. Sit here till it becomes light," whispered Ordulio. "And then go to the highway. Don't go near the house. Take care they don't see you, if you value your life!"

Roberto stared at Ordulio. There was so much he wanted to say, to ask. "Ordulio . . . what . . . ?"

But Ordulio had already pushed the canoe away from the shore. He paddled off noiselessly and disappeared into the darkness.

Roberto stood alone on the plantation. He thought of the four canoes that he had seen for an instant. The words of Ordulio sounded in his ears. "Take care they don't see you." Had the men in the canoes paddled into this creek too? Who were they? The weapons smugglers? They couldn't be anyone else.

Carefully Roberto picked his way through the plantation. It was very still. The moonlight filtered through the broad leaves of the banana plants onto the uneven ground. Roberto tried to follow the course of the creek as much as possible, but the terrain was hilly. Cautiously, almost soundlessly, he crept farther and farther.

Did he hear something?

Roberto stood still. He felt the proximity of people. Quickly he sank to the ground. On his stomach he crawled up the slope of a hill and peered over the top. On the opposite side of the creek he saw, gleaming in the moonlight, the four canoes.

In one of the canoes stood a man. Another appeared from the plantation. Something heavy was thrown ashore. The man disappeared and another appeared. Busy, busy as ants they walked past each other.

Roberto's breath faltered. He recognized the place. It was where he and Felipe had seen the old boat. Only the dry ditch was transformed by the flood tide into a gurgling creek. The path the men followed led to Manuel el Bobo's yard.

Roberto slithered carefully backward, got up, and sneaked off in a big circuit to the edge of the moonlit yard. There he stood in the shadow of the bushes and peered about. A big truck stood at the edge of the plantation. Men came along the trodden path between the bushes. Quickly and silently they shoved their load into the waiting truck.

"We're about ready. That's the lot," Roberto heard a man say.

"Right. Then shove the bananas in and get the hell out of here. . . ."

Great bunches of bananas, alternating with loose banana leaves, were hastily loaded into the truck. The door of the truck was closed. The motor started. The big truck, piled high with bananas, drove out of the yard. It presented the familiar image of a truck that takes produce to the markets early in the morning.

A group of men remained standing in the shadow of the plantation. "So," Roberto heard a voice say, "and now we'll speak a word to that drunken sot of a father of yours. Or do you think I'm going to do all the dirty work?"

The man who had spoken these words detached himself from the group and took a few steps in the direction of the house. Roberto could scarcely suppress a cry. There before him in the yard, in the full moonlight, stood old Josué! Dazed Roberto looked after him. He saw him walk hastily toward the house and enter it. The rest of the group followed meekly. Roberto recognized Pepe and guessed that the six other fellows were the remaining sons of Manuel el Bobo.

Silently Roberto withdrew among the banana plants. He made a large circle around the yard and the house and continued far into the plantation till he neared the highway.

Then he began to run. He ran until he got to the highway. He went on running in the direction of Buenaventura. He ran till he could go no farther, and panting, with his hand pressed to his side, he rested at the side of the road.

A big truck approached him from behind. The bright

headlights could be seen from afar. Roberto put up his hand. The truck rushed past. Another truck came from the opposite direction. Again Roberto raised his hand. The truck stopped.

"Want a lift?" asked the driver.

"You'll have to turn back right away," said Roberto. He was pulling at the door of the truck. "You must go back to the customs post."

"Back to the customs? You're crazy. I've just been there," said the driver. He bent forward and looked at Roberto searchingly.

"You wouldn't be the boy they've all been looking for?" he asked slowly.

"Yes," said Roberto. "I suppose I am. But we've got to go back to the customs immediately. There's a truck full of weapons on the way to Cali. Hurry!" He had finally got the truck door open and crawled up beside the driver.

"A truck full of weapons?" the driver repeated, amazed.

"Yes, and with bananas," said Roberto.

"Weapons or bananas, what is it?" asked the driver impatiently.

"Both," said Roberto. "Drive off now!"

The rest all happened like a dream. They got to the customs post. Roberto talked. The officers asked questions. He answered. They telephoned to Buenaventura, to Cali, again to Buenaventura. Roberto's parents were notified. His father came to fetch him. His mother put him to bed. Emperatriz walked exclaiming through the house, "How is it possible? Avé María. How can it be? Virgen Santísima!"

Incessantly the telephone rang.

From very far away Roberto heard them say that on the way to Cali a truck with weapons had been stopped, a truck that delivered bananas from the plantation of Manuel el Bobo!

15

THE TALK WITH DON LUÍS

Felipe came running excitedly into Roberto's room.

"Have you heard!" he shouted. "They got them! All of them! Manuel el Bobo and his whole family! My father wants to talk to you. But first tell me what happened to you! We were all so worried. The whole of Buenaventura has been looking for you. There were rumors that you'd stowed away on a freighter and. . . ."

The door opened, and Doña María entered the room. She stood by the bed and looked at her son. Roberto sat on the edge of his bed. He was still exhausted and worn out; his face was lean, there were dark rings under his eyes, and his hair needed cutting.

Doña María suppressed a sigh. It was unfortunate that Don Luís had come so early to question Roberto. She had wanted him to sleep late. But Felipe had rushed into Roberto's room before she could stop him. And Don Luís wanted to know as soon as possible what had happened. He sat waiting impatiently in Don Pablo's study.

"How are you, Roberto? Did you sleep well?" she asked anxiously.

"Like a log," answered Roberto. When he saw that his mother still looked anxious, he smiled reassuringly. "I feel a lot better than last night."

"Don Luís is here. He wants to speak to you. But. . . ."

Roberto brushed the long hair out of his eyes with an impatient gesture. "I'm coming." He got up and stretched. Doña María waited a little longer. Then she quietly left the room, softly pulling the door shut behind her.

"Boy, are you *important,*" said Felipe, who had scarcely been able to contain himself. "You may have to be a witness, you know! And you may have to go and identify the smugglers!"

"Oh no," said Roberto, frightened. "I hope I never have to see them again."

"They can't harm you," said Felipe encouragingly.

"No, perhaps not," answered Roberto.

Quickly he went to the study, followed by Felipe. Around the table sat Doña María, Don Pablo, and Don Luís.

"So, Roberto," said Don Luís, when he saw him. "There was some excitement last night. You must have heard that we detained a truck with weapons? Manuel el Bobo and his sons have been arrested, as well as the driver of their truck."

Roberto nodded. "And old Josué?" he asked.

"Old Josué?" Don Luís asked, surprised. "What do you mean?"

"Didn't you catch old Josué? He was with those men."

"But old Josué hasn't come in yet with his boats," said Don Pablo. He looked from his son to Don Luís.

"We haven't seen old Josué," said Don Luís slowly. "Are you sure he's involved in this business? You must be careful with your accusations. You know that, don't you?"

Roberto nodded. "I saw him clearly, standing in the moonlight in the yard of Manuel el Bobo, after they brought the weapons from the canoes to the truck."

"How did you know they had come to the plantation with their arms?" asked Don Luís.

"I saw them," answered Roberto. "They were paddling four canoes, single file, through the jungle into a creek that goes to the plantation, almost to their yard."

"And how did you get into the jungle?"

"With . . . oh, with old Josué," said Roberto. He wanted to bite his tongue. The other name had almost slipped out.

"With old Josué?" echoed Don Luís, astonished. "You aren't going to tell me that old Josué took you to the jungle to teach you the secrets of weapon smuggling?"

"No, no," said Roberto hastily. "It wasn't like that. I mean . . . I went with old Josué into the jungle, and then he abandoned me."

"What!" Doña María cried, aghast.

"The scoundrel!" said Don Pablo furiously.

"But . . ." began Felipe.

"I'll do the questioning," his father interrupted him. "So old Josué took you into the jungle, you say. Why did he do that?"

"I really took him into the jungle," said Roberto. The grown-ups looked uncomprehendingly at one another.

"Perhaps you would like to explain to us calmly and clearly what exactly happened," said Don Luís at last.

Roberto began to relate his experience in Ling Pa's warehouse. He repeated the conversation that he had heard there as accurately as possible. Felipe's mouth fell open with surprise.

"Why didn't you tell me all that?" he asked in an injured voice.

"I hadn't a chance. When I arrived at the pier, you were already halfway up the bay. If you had waited for me, nothing would have happened. I almost didn't get back at all."

"It was all David's fault," said Felipe lightly. "He fell out of the coconut tree and broke his leg. Someone from La Bocana came to tell us. Mother wanted to go back to Cali immediately, and in the uproar we forgot about you."

"I learned only the next day that you had left for Cali," said Doña María quietly. "At first I thought that Roberto had gone with you without telling me. But later. . . ." Her voice shook, and she put her hand to her forehead as if to stop her thoughts.

Don Luís coughed. He said, "To get back to your story, Roberto. Do you have any idea who those fellows were among the sacks in the store?"

Roberto hesitated a moment. Then he said slowly, "I'm certain now that one of them was old Josué. He heard Ling Pa mention my name and followed me to the pier."

"Did you meet him there?"

Roberto nodded. "He sat on a bench, and I told him everything I had heard. And I said I'd like to go into the jungle . . . and . . . and. . . ." Roberto stopped talking, confused. He couldn't imagine that he had ever wanted to chase smugglers in the jungle.

"And how did old Josué react?" asked Don Luís impatiently.

"He said in the end that he would not let me go alone. So we paddled together, each in a canoe, into the jungle," answered Roberto. "We went to Red Lake. Old Josué stayed awhile with his canoe on the opposite shore, so he would have a better vantage point, he said. When I searched for him the next morning, he had gone. Two days I waited for him, and at last I thought an accident had happened to him, and I was afraid. . . ." Roberto's voice began to tremble.

"The villain," said Don Pablo. "He left you there to your fate and went back in the night with the floodtide. He was at the factory the next morning early, as if nothing was wrong. A day later he calmly sailed away, while Roberto sat there alone. It's a wonder the boy survived."

"Yes," said Don Luís seriously. "That must have been old Josué's plan. Roberto had heard too much so he had to disappear."

A deep silence followed these words.

"What happened next?" asked Don Luís after a while.

"I went alone into the jungle until I got caught in the mire. And then. . . ." Roberto fell silent.

"Yes," Don Luís urged. "What happened then?"

"Oh, it was awful. I was hungry and afraid. I didn't know . . . I thought . . . I felt. . . ." stammered Roberto.

"Like a condemned man in the death house," said Felipe helpfully.

Roberto was grateful to Felipe for this remark, but Don Luís said, "You be quiet. Go on with your story, Roberto."

"Well, there in the rain forest I saw the four canoes," said Roberto.

"But you only spent two days at the lake," said Don

Luís. "And it's been two weeks since you left Buenaventura. Did you wander eleven days in the jungle alone?" He looked fixedly at Roberto, and Roberto averted his eyes.

He stared straight ahead. In his mind loomed Ordulio's gray, emaciated face as he had first seen it in the swamp. He had felt no joy when Ordulio found him. Yet the oppressive fear of loneliness left him. A limitless gratitude had overwhelmed him when he recognized Ordulio. No, no, Roberto wanted to shout. I wasn't alone. Ordulio was with me. He saved me! But he remained silent.

"Eleven days, Luís," said Don Pablo slowly. "Now that I think about it, the time fits. The shrimp boats make journeys of ten to fourteen days, so old Josué could go calmly on his fishing business and in between smuggle weapons. If you are doing something illegal, you must act as normally as possible so no one will suspect you."

Don Luís looked at Don Pablo. "And on the open sea he has every opportunity to take weapons on board as well as shrimps."

"Exactly," said Don Pablo. "That's what I meant."

"But you said old Josué wasn't in yet with his boats."

"He's been gone more than ten days, and I expect his boats any day. If he was on the plantation yesterday evening as Roberto says, then I think he must have arrived at the coast earlier. Apparently they take the weapons from the coast through the jungle."

"Yes," said Don Luís. "That's the way it must have been. They're a clever bunch."

"The only thing I don't understand is why old Josué was willing to leave his boat."

"I do," said Roberto quickly. "Manuel el Bobo and his sons were supposed to bring the weapons to the plantation. But Manuel el Bobo was drunk. That's why old Josué had to lead the convoy through the jungle. He was furious. I saw him go to scold Manuel el Bobo."

Don Pablo shook his head. "The *Villeta,* the *Buga,* and the *Pereira* in the smuggling business! It's almost unbelievable!"

"Who were on those boats?" asked Don Luís.

"The *Buga* and the *Pereira* were under the command of his two sons. They had a Japanese crew, who very conveniently couldn't speak a word of Spanish. On the *Villeta* old Josué sailed with his two younger sons. Lately they've had a Japanese engineer. Before that it was a young man from the highlands who had the job. What was his name again? Oh yes, Ordulio!"

Roberto started when he heard Ordulio's name. He felt himself blush, but no one looked at him.

"Ordulio, isn't he the fellow who's wanted for murder?"

Roberto dared not look up. Wanted . . . because of murder. How awful that sounded! And he, Roberto, knew where the murderer was. He knew Ordulio's hiding place, the miserable hut where Ordulio had brought him . . . from the swamp. . . .

Don Pablo nodded. "Yes," he said. "Too bad. I rather like that young fellow."

"You, too, Roberto," said Felipe. "You liked him too. He was repairing your outboard motor when the police came, remember?"

"Yes, yes," said Roberto hurriedly. Quickly he added, "And in the night the motor was stolen."

"It wasn't stolen," Don Pablo interrupted his son testily. "It's lying neatly packed in the attic. But you shouldn't let the night watchman take care of your things. You should look after them yourself, do you hear?"

Roberto and Felipe stared at each other, dumbfounded. At last Roberto echoed, "Not stolen?"

But Don Pablo had already turned toward Don Luís. "It's a mystery to me that no weapons were ever found on board the *Villeta,* the *Buga,* or the *Pereira,*" he said. "The boats are regularly inspected in the bay and at sea within territorial limits. Where can they have hidden them?"

"Now we've got this far, we'll hear the rest soon enough," Don Luís answered grimly.

16

THE SHIP'S GRAVEYARD

There was silence in the room. Noises from outside came faintly into the house. At the wharf a truck tooted. A woman was singing the praises of her wares in the street.

Roberto said, "It's funny they didn't find old Josué. He was at the plantation last night."

"Probably he went back to his boat as soon as possible," said Don Pablo. "As I said, his protection lies in behaving as naturally as possible."

Don Luís struck the table with his flat hand. "Our advantage is that he doesn't know what we discovered last night," he said sternly. "I promise you, he'll have a bad time when he sets foot on shore. Do you know, Pablo, I thought. . . ?" Don Luís cut short his sentence. His eyes slid toward the two boys, who were listening attentively.

"You can go now, boys. For the present I don't need Roberto anymore. Oh, that reminds me, Felipe. I promised your mother I'd go to La Bocana to look for her watch. She's lost it and thinks she left it there. I have no time now, and it's a good job for the two of you. You may find a boat going out to La Bocana. Otherwise, you may rent one."

Felipe disliked being dismissed so summarily, but Roberto got up eagerly, glad to leave the room.

It was oppressively hot outside, hotter than usual. Like a damp woolen blanket the clouds hung over the town. There wasn't a breath of wind. The palms in the park stood motionless. The bay looked like molten lead.

"What do you think of that?" Felipe burst out suddenly.

"Of what?" asked Roberto absently.

"Sending us away like small boys!"

Roberto said nothing, and Felipe looked at him with irritation. "You act as if you don't care . . . while you . . . if they hadn't had you. . . ." He shrugged his shoulders. "I don't understand you," he said, hurt. "First you're eager to go after the smugglers. And now that they're planning in your own house to capture the rest of the gang, you've suddenly lost interest. Just when it gets exciting!"

"They can sort it out themselves. I did my bit," said Roberto dryly.

"Come on. Was it as bad as that? Is it true what they say about the jungle? You can tell me."

Tell! thought Roberto bitterly. Tell! If only I could tell! For one moment he longed to share his adventures with someone, to tell Felipe everything, everything: his stay in the jungle, the loneliness, the long, useless waiting, the fears, Ordulio. . . .

"Well, do as you like. I don't really care." Felipe kicked away a stone. It fell with a splash into the water. They had reached the pier. A little boat was on the point of departure for La Bocana. It was full of women who had been marketing. They had made purchases for the following Sunday, when the visitors would come to La Bocana. They had great overflowing baskets on their laps, before their feet and beside them, on the benches. The passengers were waiting resignedly till the boat had been filled to the last available inch and could set out.

The tide was rising. They went against it, and the green shores slowly slid past. Felipe grumbled about the weather, the full boat, the dull journey. Roberto scarcely heard him. His thoughts were with that morning's conversation. For some reason it had left a bitter taste. He had an unsatisfied feeling, a gnawing feeling of . . . what was it? thought Roberto. What was the reason for his anxiety?

He did not know.

Thoughtfully he watched the water stream away behind the boat, the foaming wake left by the churning propeller. The motor throbbed. It had a regular, monotonous rhythm, always the same dark, repetitious syllables: Or-du-li-o, Or-du-li-o.

Beside him Felipe sighed. "Good! We've arrived! Are you coming, Roberto? I must say you haven't been much company."

The boat shoved against the wobbly landing stage. The passengers stepped ashore. The women dispersed, disappearing with their loaded baskets into their dingy huts, which bore the proud name of *Restaurant*.

The boys walked over the black strand to the bungalow. They found Pedro busily chopping wood. When he saw the boys, he looked up in surprise. "How did you two get here?" he asked.

"By boat, how else?" said Felipe, still feeling out of sorts. "Mother has lost her watch. She thinks she left it here. Have you found it?"

Pedro shrugged his shoulders. "I don't know anything about it," he said. "You'll have to ask Marta. But it's a bad day to come here." He shook his head.

"Why?" asked Felipe. "It's just a day, like all the others."

Pedro lowered the corners of his mouth and again

shook his head. "It's a bad day," he said. "A storm is coming."

"A storm?" asked Felipe. "I've never seen it so calm."

"Ah!" muttered Pedro. "You said it." He straightened his old back and stared out over the ocean. The boys followed his glance. The sea was frighteningly calm. The sky had a dirty, pale yellow color. Far in the northwest dark clouds were massing.

"I don't like it," said Pedro. "If I were you, I wouldn't search too long for that watch. I'd go home as soon as possible." He began to chop again.

The boys entered the bungalow, looking for Marta. They found her in her smoke-filled kitchen and repeated their question.

"Your mother's watch? No, I haven't seen it. It might still be in one of the bedrooms, which I locked when the family left." With a sigh Marta shuffled into the cubbyhole she shared with Pedro and came back with the keys.

She unlocked the various doors. The little bedrooms showed signs of having been hastily vacated. There was a mess everywhere. Nothing had been tidied. Marta had not overworked herself. The shutters were closed tightly; the little rooms were stuffy and dark. There was a musty smell. Hastily the boys threw open the shutters and began to search. Felipe felt along a ridge of the windowsill, and his fingers closed down on the watch.

"I've got it," he told Roberto.

"Good," said Roberto. "Shall we ask Marta if she can give us something to drink? I'm terribly thirsty."

"Me too," said Felipe. "It's muggy, isn't it?" They left the room and went to the porch. Outside it was still as a tomb. The world around them was bathed in a queer yellow light.

Pedro and Marta stood on the beach and watched a few boats that were moving toward the mouth of the bay.

"They're trying to enter it before the storm breaks," said Pedro to the boys. "They're doing the right thing."

They all followed the boats with their eyes.

Roberto nudged Felipe. "They are the boats of old Josué, don't you see? That is the *Buga* and that one the *Pereira,* and the last one, lagging behind, is the *Villeta.* How strange!"

"Why funny?" asked Felipe. "Your father said they could be putting in any moment and here they are."

"But I've never seen them return in that order. The *Villeta* with old Josué always comes first. Always. I. . . ." Roberto wasn't able to finish his sentence. A bright streak of lightning split the sky, followed by a growling thunderclap, which seemed to come out of the sea itself.

The water suddenly heaved into motion. A tremor went through the palms and bushes on the beach. All the doors and shutters of the bungalow began to rattle.

"The shutters! Quick!" shouted Pedro. Before they had properly closed and fastened them, the storm broke in all its fury. The wind keened over the beach, around the bungalow, through the jungle. The lightning was never out of the sky. The sea looked black. High waves beat over the beach. The *Buga* and the *Pereira* had vanished around the headland and would be in the bay. But far out at sea the *Villeta* was struggling with the waves.

Groups of people stood on the beach in the whirling sand. Little naked children clutched the flapping skirts of their mothers and peered at the boat.

"It should have been in long ago," Pedro shouted into the wind. "I don't understand what's the matter with it! The boat won't make it at that rate!"

They stared across the heaving water, straining to see, until tears came to their eyes. As far as they could see, the boat was making no headway nor was it drifting away. It didn't seem to move.

"It's not advancing!" cried Roberto.

"Avé María, it's on a reef!" shouted Pedro.

Slowly it dawned on everybody that the *Villeta* was in trouble. Women began to wail. Men paced back and forth on the shore, gesticulating wildly. Children shouted. Anxiously the people stared at the boat.

High waves beat over its deck. In that wild water the little vessel looked like a lonely floating bird. Lightning split the sky; heavy thunderbolts followed one after the other in deafening succession. The storm wind whipped over the ocean. The water looked like a boiling witch's caldron.

Time passed. A small boat left the bay and sailed toward the helpless vessel.

"The lifeboat is on the way!" shouted Felipe. They

followed the lifesaving craft with their eyes. It danced on the waves, disappeared, and bobbed up again in the gigantic mountain landscape of water.

The thunder was drifting away, but the wind increased, lashing up the waves. A sigh of relief came from the people on the beach when the lifeboat finally reached the *Villeta*. The two boats melted into a black blot among the waves. The water spray prevented anyone from seeing what was happening.

After a while the lifeboat returned. Gradually the distance between the small crowded boat and the abandoned *Villeta* became greater. Bravely the little lifeboat fought its way back to the bay.

The storm wind whipped the water higher and higher up the narrow beach. The people were driven back. Pedro and Marta sought protection in the kitchen behind the bungalow. Felipe and Roberto went to the porch. Leaning over its wobbly railing, they kept staring at the boiling waves, the slowly approaching lifeboat, and the helpless derelict on the reef.

Then they saw the canoe. Behind the lifeboat, between the coast and the abandoned vessel, danced a canoe. It had one man in it! They could hardly believe their eyes.

"Roberto, do you see that?" shouted Felipe.

"But it's . . . it's old Josué," Roberto yelled back.

"What? Roberto, that's impossible. You must be mistaken."

"No, no. I see him. I'm certain," shouted Roberto.

He shivered. The picture of old Josué in his canoe had been so indelibly engraved in his memory that he would have recognized it anywhere.

Spellbound, the boys watched the man in the canoe desperately fighting the waves.

"Roberto, he's going to the *Villeta*!"

Roberto nodded silently. He also had seen that old Josué was making a superhuman attempt to reach his boat.

"But that's crazy!"

"Yes, it's incredible."

They kept watching. The waves threw the little canoe up in the air. For a moment it trembled on a curling comber, then it disappeared in a deep trough, only to be swung up again the next moment.

Felipe clutched at Roberto. "If we could only signal the lifeboat!"

But the lifeboat had already left the little canoe far behind and was approaching the mouth of the bay. The canoe vanished behind a green wall of water, emerged, and vanished again. Again it was lifted up by the foaming waves in a cruel and endless game.

Far away lay the *Villeta,* defenseless. The coral reefs bit into her sides. The sea clawed at her. High waves washed the deck. The boat was already beginning to list. Then it began to rain. Streams of water splashed down. The wind moaned across the sea. It chased the rain over the water, whistled through the jungle, and wailed around the miserable huts along the strand. The sea roared.

The boys were drenched in a minute on the open porch. But, shivering, they remained standing in the raging wind, until the dense curtain of rain erased the canoe and the *Villeta* from their sight.

17

NIGHT OVER BUENAVENTURA

All of Buenaventura was in an uproar. The whole town talked about the smugglers, the storm, the wreck of the *Villeta*. In Don Pablo's house the telephone shrilled constantly all during the next day. Everyone wanted to know the details of what had happened.

Now it was evening, and Roberto sat alone on the

porch. He gazed into the silent garden and the street. After the storm of the day before nature had returned to rest. The slender palms were etched against the starlit sky. The night wind rustled in the dark crowns. Fireflies sparkled up above the long grass of the front garden, glowed a moment in the blue twilight, then disappeared. The earth smelled good after the heavy rain.

Roberto fidgeted on his chair. He rose and sat down again. What was the matter with him? He still had that uncomfortable feeling, a vague sensation of anxiety. The day before, when Don Luís talked about Ordulio, this feeling had come over him, a gnawing feeling of doubt.

Doubt. That was it!

What had Don Luís said? "Ordulio, isn't he the young man who's wanted for murder?"

And he, Roberto, had remained quiet. But he could not say anything. He had given Ordulio his word.

Ordulio forced me to; he made use of the circumstances, thought Roberto. No, that wasn't true. Ordulio had not forced him. He had promised Ordulio freely, because he wanted to go home, because he was afraid. But that was not quite true either.

Roberto thought of the man with whom he had wandered through the forest, with whom he had shared the primitive food, the man who had stayed behind alone in the jungle. Notwithstanding everything, there had been comradeship. He had promised to hold his tongue out of fear but also out of loyalty to his rescuer. And now?

Footsteps sounded in the sitting room. Don Pablo

flicked on the light and came onto the porch with a newspaper under his arm. "Ah, you're out here," he said. He took a chair, sat down beside Roberto, and began to read.

Roberto shifted on his chair and swung his leg. "Father," he said at last.

"Mmm, yes?" answered his father without looking up.

"If someone has committed a murder and later saves someone's life, what happens then?"

Don Pablo lowered his paper. "What do you mean, what then?" he asked, surprised.

"Do you think he still should be punished?"

"You mean, can he make amends by exchanging a life for a life? No, Roberto, that's not what happens. It's not that simple. No one can be his own judge."

"And if someone . . . eh . . . protects a murderer?"

"Ah, then he violates the law and could be punished. From a purely human point of view I'd like to add that the punishment is not as important as his conscience. A person must act honorably according to his conscience. You understand?"

"Yes," said Roberto, "I understand that. But. . . ." There was the difficulty, he thought. His honor told him to hold his tongue, but his conscience was troubled. He felt uncertain and irritated. Deep in his heart he blamed Ordulio for getting him into the difficulty. And at the same time he realized that he was unreasonable. He tried to think objectively about Ordulio, to remember the days in the marsh, their last conversation, but the picture was muddied. He recalled Ordulio with mixed feelings.

In the rain forest the situation had seemed so simple. Now he was home again his attitude had changed, just as Ordulio had predicted.

"Besides punishment is relative," his father continued.

"What do you mean?"

The telephone rang. Emperatriz came in with a scowl from the kitchen. Her feet slapped angrily on the tiled floor. "I'm going crazy with the telephone in this house," she snapped.

"A ver," she shouted into the mouthpiece.

"Who is it?" asked Roberto.

But Emperatriz did not answer. She was listening attentively. Her face relaxed. "Aníbal!" she cried. "Aníbal, is it really you?" There followed a long conversation. When she put down the receiver, she had an expression of mingled joy and indignation on her face.

"My poor brother! He has had such a bad time, Dios *mío,* and it is all the fault of Ling Pa, that scoundrel! If he had not talked Aníbal into smuggling whiskey, then the customs people would not have suspected him of smuggling weapons. And Ling Pa let them think it, so he wouldn't be suspected himself. The hypocrite! Oh, how Aníbal has suffered and worried. That poor fellow!"

Emperatriz wiped her eyes elaborately and disappeared into the kitchen, shaking her head.

"See?" said Don Pablo. "That's what I mean. If Aníbal had not fled, the customs people would have known earlier that Aníbal had nothing to do with the weapons business. By escaping punishment, he brought greater difficulties on himself."

Roberto wanted to say something, but Doña María entered the room and the telephone rang again.

"That was Luís," said Doña María to her husband. "He is on his way here. Felipe is coming too, Roberto."

Before long Don Luís's car stopped in front of the gate. Don Pablo went to meet him. Roberto brought more chairs.

"Well," said Don Luís, when they were all seated. "I believe this business is about taken care of. I still have to ask you a few questions, Roberto. But the principal things we know. Old Josué was not the originator of the weapons smuggling, but he was the inspiration of the men. When he was gone, they all confessed, one by one. To help themselves, they betrayed the others and told all they knew. They're a noble lot, I must say. Well, they've all been arrested except one."

"Who is that?" asked Roberto.

"The organizer. But we know who he is and where he lives. We've already asked the American government to start extradition proceedings."

"Is he an American?" asked Roberto, surprised.

"No. He's the owner of the plantation where Manuel el Bobo was overseer, but he lives in the United States. Whenever he came here, to pay his people and to control his business, he did so under the guise of an American tourist."

"The man in the bright shirt, who lost his wallet on the bridge!" cried Roberto.

"The man who lay senseless on the beach and later disappeared," Felipe added. "I still wonder how that was possible."

"I'll tell you," said Don Luís. "When you were cheerfully canoeing along the coast, the boats of old Josué had just unloaded weapons in a small inlet. It was the first time they had tried this route, and they made a big mistake. It was shortly after the new moon, and they hadn't counted on the spring tide. The ebb tide was so low that one of the boats got into difficulties. The organizer was there to see if the new plan of transporting the weapons through the jungle was feasible. When he saw you, he went to meet you. He faked the accident to prevent you from going farther. After you had gone off to get help, he got up and canoed back to supervise the rest of the transfer."

"Why did he go himself? Why didn't he send one of his men?" asked Roberto. Don Luís smiled. "Because the people on the plantation and the crew of the boats ran the chance of being recognized by someone from Buenaventura. The organizer had not been in contact with many people."

Felipe began to laugh. "He must have cursed himself for giving you those fifty dollars, Roberto. If he hadn't done that, he wouldn't have made such an impression on you."

But Roberto had another thought. "Perhaps he was the one who was talking with old Josué in Ling Pa's warehouse," he said.

"Indeed," answered Don Luís. "That's what we think."

"I'm surprised that Ling Pa never noticed what was going on in his warehouse," said Felipe. "I thought he was so intelligent."

"I'm sure Ling Pa suspected something," said Don Luís. "He kept quiet, hoping to profit from it. Or perhaps he had too much on his own conscience and preferred to notice nothing."

Emperatriz had just brought the coffee. She sniffed disdainfully when she heard Ling Pa's name.

"If that route through the jungle was something new," said Don Pablo, "how did they land the weapons before?"

"For a long time they were simply unloaded at the landing stage of your factory, Pablo," answered Don Luís amiably.

Don Pablo stared at him in consternation. "What?" he shouted. "At my factory? How dare they!"

"It was the simplest way for them. You have to admit that the distance from your factory to the plantation is much less than from the coast to the plantation, and the Dagua River is more navigable than the jungle. Unfortunately for them, the authorities made using your pier too risky."

Roberto and Felipe exchanged a significant look. "The canoe that shot up the river," whispered Felipe.

"The boats of old Josué were at the dock then," muttered Roberto.

"And we, silly asses, thought someone had gone off with the motor."

"I'd like to know why no weapons were ever found on board the boats. They were inspected, weren't they?" asked Don Pablo testily.

"My dear Pablo," answered Don Luís. "The weapons lay at the bottom of the tanks, under the shrimps, the seawater, and the ice! They were wrapped in plastic. In one of the tanks of the *Buga* we found a rifle, packed beautifully so that it was watertight. The gentlemen had forgotten to unload it after their last expedition. But I don't criticize them for it! It's a marvelous piece of evidence."

Don Luís was silent for a moment. Then he went on, "I do have to admit that they were well organized. It was a sort of family affair. Manuel el Bobo and his sons took care of the transportation over land, and old Josué and his sons of the transportation over sea. The Japanese crew just sweated; they had nothing to fear from them."

Felipe said dryly, "And what about Ordulio, Roberto?"

Roberto was startled. "What . . . what do you mean?" he stammered.

"Ordulio sailed on the *Villeta,*" said Felipe. "He must have known what was going on. Yet he never told."

"That's true," said Don Luís.

Don Pablo slapped the table with the flat of his hand.

"Shall I tell you something? Old Josué knew all along what Ordulio had done. Don't think that old devil left anything to chance. He had Ordulio completely in his power. Ordulio was forced to keep quiet."

He didn't even tell me, thought Roberto. What had gone on in Ordulio's mind when he fell into the hands of old Josué? How had he felt when he had been put to the choice of playing along or of being arrested?

Roberto did not know. He had slept with Ordulio under the same roof, shared his meager food, but he knew nothing about Ordulio's feelings or thoughts. For the first time he thought of Ordulio as a lonely person.

Roberto had asked help from Ordulio when he needed him and had made use of his services. He would never forget the moment when he had recognized Ordulio in the swamps. That blessed moment, when he wasn't alone anymore.

But after he had got over the terrible experience of being alone in the jungle, he was afraid again. Afraid for his own safety. Was he justified in feeling threatened by Ordulio?

Certainly Ordulio had changed. He had been stiff and defensive. But why had Roberto distrusted him? When had Ordulio ever done him harm? The stay in the jungle had left its mark on Ordulio. He had been nervous, tense, and curt. There had been a strained relationship between them. But that wasn't completely Ordulio's fault.

Roberto had to admit to himself that he was at fault too. He had been thinking only of himself. He had been interested only in his own fate, afraid for his own safety. Not once had he looked at the situation from Ordulio's point of view. Not once had he tried to understand Ordulio's difficulties. Roberto bit his lips. He felt ashamed.

Around him the talk continued.

Don Pablo repeated with emphasis, "I tell you, those gentlemen left nothing to chance. They even made a clever use of the tide!"

Felipe looked at him inquiringly. "How? What do you mean?"

"Old Josué's boats took in the weapons while they were out at sea, fishing. Before they entered the bay they put them on shore. Manuel el Bobo and his sons had to transport them through the jungle, in their canoes, from the coast to the plantation. This had to be done in the evening, when the tide was rising and in their favor. They had calculated it so that they would enter the plantation at high tide. We all know that the difference between ebb tide and flood tide on our coast is very great. But we don't always realize that some places which seem dry most of the day can be reached by water when the flood is at its highest."

Felipe nodded thoughtfully. "That's why Manuel el Bobo's son wanted us out of the way when Roberto and I stood looking at the boat," he said. "There was no water there then, but the tide was rising. He didn't want us to stay around too long and discover the creek."

He added meditatively, "But I don't understand why old Josué wasn't on board the *Villeta* yesterday morning.

What was he doing in a canoe, on the sea, in such a storm!"

"We'll never know exactly what happened," answered Don Luís. "As Roberto told us, old Josué went angrily into Manuel el Bobo's house after they had loaded the weapons in the truck. The two men got into a terrible argument, as I heard later. It cost Manuel a few teeth and old Josué his precious time. When he went back, the water was falling. He must have had trouble getting away from the plantation. He may have got stuck in the jungle. Whatever happened, the *Villeta* waited as long as possible for him. But when old Josué did not come, she had to put to sea without him. She had to be away from the coast before low tide. They intended to go back later to pick him up, but the threatening storm prevented that. When old Josué finally appeared in the little inlet, the *Villeta* was not there anymore. He paddled along the coast till he saw his boats. The *Villeta* was sailing in the wake of the others, but it was no use. Without Josué the *Villeta* was like a ship without a rudder." Don Luís paused.

"Old Josué must have seen sooner than anyone else that the *Villeta* was in trouble. He threw all caution to the winds and tried to reach his boat. The storm caught him at sea. . . ." Don Luís fell silent.

Roberto thought of old Josué as he had last seen him, fighting the waves. Had the canoe capsized? Had old Josué reached his ship before it went down? No one would ever know.

Don Luís took a last swallow of his cold coffee. He put down his cup and coughed. "Since we are talking about that day on the plantation, Roberto," he said, "something still bothers me. You told me you saw four canoes going through the jungle."

"Yes," said Roberto. "There were four."

"Exactly," said Don Luís with emphasis. "But when you arrived at the plantation, there should have been five canoes. Old Josué took one to paddle back to the coast. There should have been four canoes left on the plantation. We found only three."

"Perhaps they didn't know how to look," said Felipe.

Don Luís ignored this remark. "I think it's strange," he said. "But perhaps Roberto has an explanation." He looked sharply at Roberto. Roberto felt himself stiffen. He tried to avoid the piercing glance, but couldn't. The eyes of Don Luís remained focused on him. They held Roberto's eyes prisoner. They undermined Roberto's will. They looked as if they could read his thoughts.

Ordulio, thought Roberto despairingly. Everyone looked at him. An oppressive silence reigned on the porch.

"Well," said Don Luís. "What have you got to say?"

Ordulio, Ordulio! No, no, not *that*! Roberto felt defenseless under that compelling glance. The commanding voice was forcing him to speak. His resistance was breaking. Tears jumped into his eyes. He blinked them away. He looked helplessly around and met his father's eyes.

Did his father understand that there had been something in his son's life that he could not talk about? Not yet anyhow?

Don Pablo said, "Let's not worry about that little detail, Luís. The main thing is that the smuggling band has been broken up."

Don Luís relaxed. His eyes left Roberto and met those of Don Pablo. He began to stroke his face with a tired gesture. "You're right," he said. "My task is done."

Doña María and Don Pablo walked with Don Luís and Felipe to the gate. In the dark garden the fireflies winked, a cricket chirped, the wind stirred the palm leaves.

Roberto remained alone on the porch, staring into the tropical night. He had an uneasy feeling that this evening was not the end, more like a beginning. He would have trouble with his conscience from time to time. Ordulio!

He had crossed an invisible barrier into the adult world, a twilight wasteland, not unlike the shadowy rain forest where he had wandered, a world where one could never be entirely sure. He stood tense, almost reluctant. Roberto knew that he could not draw back anymore into the lost world of the past. He had to grow up. It would take time for him to understand that his experience had made him richer, that it had helped him to mature.

From far up the estuary came the whistle of a freighter. Above the dark crowns of the palms the moon was coming up, silvering the little town at the meeting of the rivers. Its beams drew a broad, gleaming trail over the water. It made the jungle, at its border, look still darker.

Siny R. van Iterson was born in the Netherlands Antilles, on the island of Curaçao, and has traveled extensively. For short periods she has lived in many different places, including Europe, the United States, Central and South America, and the Caribbean. Interested in writing from her earliest years, she first worked on a newspaper and later began to write children's books. She lives in Bogotá, Colombia.

Mrs. van Iterson is the author of a number of books published in Holland. Several of them have been translated into German and Danish.

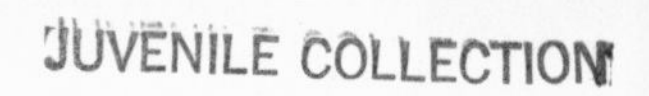